Jet Set Docs

How far will they go to find the one they love?

Introducing this season's hottest Harlequin Medical Romance novels packed with your summertime dose of dreamy doctors, pulse-racing drama and sizzling romantic tension! Fly up, up and away and follow these globe-trotting docs as they travel to stunning international destinations for work...but end up finding a special someone in their arms!

Grab your passport and find out in

Second Chance in Santiago by Tina Beckett
One Night to Sydney Wedding by JC Harroway
The Doctor's Italian Escape by Annie Claydon
Spanish Doc to Heal Her by Karin Baine
ER Doc's South Pole Reunion by Juliette Hyland
Their Accidental Vegas Vows by Amy Ruttan

All available now!

Dear Reader,

As the mother of two sons, I know parenting isn't easy. We can't get it right all of the time, but mostly we just want our children to be happy.

In this story, Inés and Ángelo have both had difficult childhoods and are estranged from their families. Circumstances force Inés back to Spain to deal with the very issues that pushed her away. Despite initially clashing with her new colleague, Ángelo, Inés soon finds they have more in common than she'd ever imagined. It's not long before he becomes as big a part of her life as he is in her parents' lives.

I hope you enjoy following their romance in the sun!

Love,

Karin xx

SPANISH DOC TO HEAL HER

KARIN BAINE

If you purchased this book without a cover you should be aware that this book is stolen property. It was reported as "unsold and destroyed" to the publisher, and neither the author nor the publisher has received any payment for this "stripped book."

MEDICAL ROMANCE

ISBN-13: 978-1-335-94315-6

Spanish Doc to Heal Her

Copyright © 2025 by Karin Baine

All rights reserved. No part of this book may be used or reproduced in any manner whatsoever without written permission.

Without limiting the author's and publisher's exclusive rights, any unauthorized use of this publication to train generative artificial intelligence (AI) technologies is expressly prohibited.

This is a work of fiction. Names, characters, places and incidents are either the product of the author's imagination or are used fictitiously. Any resemblance to actual persons, living or dead, businesses, companies, events or locales is entirely coincidental.

For questions and comments about the quality of this book, please contact us at CustomerService@Harlequin.com.

TM and ® are trademarks of Harlequin Enterprises ULC.

 Harlequin Enterprises ULC
22 Adelaide St. West, 41st Floor
Toronto, Ontario M5H 4E3, Canada
www.Harlequin.com

Printed in U.S.A.

Karin Baine lives in Northern Ireland with her husband, two sons and her out-of-control notebook collection. Her mother and her grandmother's vast collection of books inspired her love of reading and her dream of becoming a Harlequin author. Now she can tell people she has a *proper* job! You can follow Karin on X @karinbaine1 or visit her website for the latest news, karinbaine.com.

Books by Karin Baine

Harlequin Medical Romance

Carey Cove Midwives

Festive Fling to Forever

Christmas North and South

Festive Fling with the Surgeon

Royal Docs

Surgeon Prince's Fake Fiancée
A Mother for His Little Princess

Single Dad for the Heart Doctor
Falling Again for the Surgeon
Nurse's Risk with the Rebel
An American Doctor in Ireland
Midwife's One-Night Baby Surprise
Nurse's New Year with the Billionaire
Tempted by Her Off-Limits Boss

Visit the Author Profile page
at Harlequin.com for more titles.

For Mum & Dad xx

**Praise for
Karin Baine**

"Emotionally enchanting! The story was fast-paced,
emotionally charged and oh so satisfying!"
—*Goodreads* on *Their One-Night Twin Surprise*

CHAPTER ONE

INÉS DE LA FUENTE wasn't used to the sun any more. Despite her Spanish heritage, and her formative years spent living in the Costa Blanca, she'd spent the better part of a decade in London.

But it wasn't the heat, the bright glare of the sun, or even the dreaded mosquitos which were making her feel queasy about returning home to the town of Solara Vista. As she walked down the street towards the familiar family medical practice, it was the prospect of working here causing her anxiety.

Although she'd stayed in contact with her mother these past years, it had mostly been by text, with the occasional call. Actually being here was a whole different ball game. A world she thought she'd never come back to. Never wanted to come back to. Except circumstances had taken over.

She'd arrived late last night and had an awkward reunion with her mother before retiring to her old bedroom. Today was going to be a test, but she'd been through much worse recently and survived. Now she just wanted to get on with this new chapter of her life until she knew what the next one held.

Inés took a deep breath, pushed the button and waited for the intercom static to sound.

'It's me, Mama,' Inés announced herself before her mother had a chance to launch into her spiel about clinic opening times. She knew she was early. By an entire day. Because she had nowhere else to go, unable to face rattling around the family villa on her own with only the ghosts of the past to keep her company. She would rather keep busy, and start earning money. The more she managed to put away, the quicker she'd be able to move on.

The door buzzed and she pushed her way inside. Although the place had apparently been dragged into the twenty-first century, it still had that recognisable clean smell which took her right back to her not-so-happy youth.

Bright and airy, with a light turquoise and white theme, there was no trace of the old dark red walls and brass light fittings which resembled a haunted house and made her shudder even to think about. Perhaps her father had finally decided to move on from the past after all. It gave her a pang in her chest to not have been a part of that and perhaps witness a change from the intimidating man who'd dominated her life. Though she didn't regret leaving when she had. Even if she'd swapped one emotional prison for another...

Inés's father, though a brilliant doctor, had been an unrelenting parent. Strict, unyielding and determined that his daughter would follow him into medicine, on his terms. That meant there was no life for her beyond study, or joining the family business. Too suffocating for a teenage girl who had wanted a life of her own. She'd known that once she enrolled in medical school her future was mapped out for her and she'd be under his control for ever, just like her mother.

Although she had been interested in being a doctor, she had wanted her freedom and secretly applied to study in London. Her act of rebellion was the only way she could ever have the independence she longed for, though it meant leaving it until the last minute to tell them of her intentions, incurring the wrath of both of her parents. Her father, disappointed and angry that she'd disobeyed his plans for her future, had raged at her. Her mother had wept and wailed, and begged her to stay. But for once in her life, Inés had taken control and bravely moved abroad to the unknown.

Naive, lonely and a prime target for a man like Marty who had slowly taken her independence away from her again. She hadn't realised until it was too late that she'd been manipulated and gaslit for years into staying with him. He'd fed into that feeling that she had no one in her life, encouraging her to keep her distance from her family, never repairing the wounds. Until she was completely reliant on him.

It was ironic that the state of her father's health had given her the chance to start again. Though she hadn't known the extent of his illness until recently because of their estrangement, leaving Marty had also given her the courage to reach out to her mother. Her plea for Inés's help had given her somewhere to go. For now.

'Inés!' Her mother jumped up from behind the reception desk and ran over to swamp her in a hug.

'Mama.' Inés accepted her awkwardly, still not at the stage where she was ready to show any affection. After all, her mother hadn't backed her even when she'd finally stood up to her father and told him she wanted to live her own life. Instead, her mother had pleaded with her to, 'Just fall in line', and do as she was told in order to keep the peace. However, Inés wasn't like her mother and wasn't content to sacrifice her independence simply to keep her father happy and hadn't seen why she should.

Perhaps if Inés had had some support she

wouldn't have left the country altogether, but in that moment, she hadn't seen any other choice. She'd needed to get as far away as she could from her father's influence.

Looking back, she'd likely thought that she would get her relationship back with her parents once life had settled down for her. Marty had changed that. He'd been instrumental in making the estrangement permanent. Allegedly for Inés's benefit, telling her she didn't need that kind of toxicity in her life. Now she could see it was just another way of manipulating her. Making sure she had no one to turn to other than him and ensuring that she couldn't leave him. Thankfully, she'd come to her senses eventually and made her escape, regardless of not having any support.

'What are you doing here? I thought you weren't starting until tomorrow.' Even though she'd lived here for decades, Marie de la Fuente still hadn't lost her English accent. She'd met Inés's father on a girly holiday and stayed, leaving behind her job and family in London to set up home with the handsome Spaniard who'd captured her heart. Completely dependent on him. Stuck.

A story Inés knew all too well.

'I thought I should get acquainted with the place as soon as possible.' Not quite the truth.

It was hard being here when the clinic had been the main source of the conflict between her and her father. When he'd expected her to devote her life to it and didn't care what she might have wanted. But it was worse at home, where they'd had most of their rows. A place she'd come to despise because of the 'my house, my rules' adage which had been quoted ad nauseum. Where she wasn't allowed to have a voice, or an opinion, of her own. Where her father was king. Or a dictator, depending on whose point of view you listened to.

'Your father is delighted you're finally here.'

'It's only temporary,' she reminded her mother. Not wanting either of her parents to get carried away by the idea it was going to be a permanent arrangement. For now, it suited both parties for her to be here, but that would change and she wasn't committing herself to anything. That much hadn't changed in ten years.

'How is Father anyway?' Inés thought she should ask since it was partly the reason she was here. Her mother's plea for help at the practice had simply happened to coincide with her break up and subsequent homelessness.

'Not good.' Her mother sighed and seemed to visibly age before her eyes, although she hadn't really physically changed in the ten years since Inés had seen her face to face. Perhaps there were a few grey hairs and more wrinkles around the eyes, but still the same woman Inés had inherited her blue eyes and freckled nose from. It was only her thick dark hair and olive complexion which harked back to Inés's Spanish heritage. Along with her accent. Thanks to her mother, she spoke perfect English, but she was always going to stand out in London. As much as she did here. Never quite fitting into either world.

'I'm genuinely sorry to hear that.' Despite their issues, Inés didn't wish ill health on him. He was still her father after all.

She'd been shocked to find out how seriously ill he was. And riddled with guilt. So much time had passed between them, yet she'd held on to that anger towards him over the past. Now, faced with the prospect of losing him completely from her life, she was conflicted about how she felt. Perhaps if she'd broken free of Marty's control earlier, she might have reconciled with her parents. Had some sort of relationship with them. But now there wasn't much time for that to happen. There was a kind of grief in knowing that which she was still trying to work through.

'We're both so glad you came. Maybe you could visit him later?'

Inés held her hopeful mother's gaze and responded with a frown. 'I'm not ready to do that.'

14 SPANISH DOC TO HEAL HER

Her mother nodded. 'In your own time. Although I don't think he has much left...'

'So, where am I going to be working from?' Inés changed the subject before she was drawn into a possible row. She knew how seriously ill her father was, dealing with stage four heart failure. After a previous heart bypass twenty years ago, he'd finally run out of lives, his age and failing health ruling out any further medical intervention. His time was limited, but coming back to work here was totally different from Inés facing him again.

It hadn't been the altruistic move her parents likely thought it was. Nor was it entirely down to an attack of conscience and a wish for a reconciliation before he died. After coming to the realisation she needed to get away from Marty, and finally making the break, her mother's call to help out with the practice had seemed serendipitous. Only time would tell if it had been a good move for her personally.

'You can have your father's office. Ángelo is next door.'

'Ah, yes. Ángelo. I'd forgotten about him.' The sainted doctor who worked alongside her parents at the practice and who apparently could do no wrong. Inés had heard a lot about him over the years. The man who'd done everything she wouldn't and made her parents happy into the bargain. Not only replacing her in their affections, and in the practice, but also the substitute who joined them for holidays and Sunday dinners. Their surrogate son who didn't appear to have a life of his own.

Not that she was bitter. She'd been glad to get away from it all at the time, but now she was back at square one. Having left her home and her job, she was reliant on her family again and that didn't sit well with her. Especially when she'd had her taste of independence. Before Marty had done his best to steal it from her again.

Her mother led her to her father's office, which had also had a makeover since the last time she'd been here. Inés wondered if the bright modern decor had been Ángelo's idea and how he'd managed to exert any influence when she hadn't even managed to take control of her own life.

'He should be in soon. Always early, stays late. He's been our anchor. I don't know how we ever managed without him,' her mother gushed.

Inés smiled with gritted teeth. 'Why did you only come to me when Father is nearing the end? How have you coped until now?'

She'd known her father was ill, but not to what extent. It had taken her some time to get over her break up. Counselling, trying to find somewhere to stay and avoiding Marty, might have been easier if her mother had asked her to come here sooner. Though she probably wouldn't have been ready for another layer of trauma so soon after she'd made the escape. She wasn't sure she was ready for it now.

'You know your father, he kept working until he physically couldn't. Even though he'd had his own diagnosis. I didn't want you to think we were emotionally blackmailing you into coming back, but we got to a point where we needed your help. We've had temporary staff in to cover his absence, but the patients need some stability. Ángelo has worked day and night and taken on some of the load, but he can't do everything on his own.'

Inés imagined he'd tried. Though she'd never seen, or spoken, to the famous Ángelo, she already held some resentment when he seemed to go out of his way to get into her father's good books. Something which she'd never managed to do.

'Well, I'm hoping to start right now if possible.' She just wanted to do the job she was here for and hopefully the time away from her life in London would help her figure out what she was going to do next. Especially since she'd left her job.

'That's fine with me. We don't want to let any of our patients down. I'm sure they'll feel reassured that another de la Fuente is in residence.' Her mother took her hand and Inés resisted snatching it away. She still loved her mother, but it would take a while for them to heal.

Inés still held some resentment that she'd never stood up for her, but her mother had never stood up for herself either when it came to her father.

'Now is as good a time as any.' Inés set the same rucksack she'd arrived with last night on to the desk. Although today it contained her water bottle and some snacks to get her through the day, her few belongings stashed into one drawer back at the villa.

'Is that really the only luggage you have?' Her mother looked aghast once more at the battered bag she shrugged off her shoulders. It was difficult for Inés to explain why she hadn't brought much with her without going into the details of her break up and she didn't want her parents to know her new life hadn't been everything she'd wanted after all.

'I travel light. Besides, I don't know how long I'm going to be here for yet.' She'd had a home and a life in London, but in the end, all she'd wanted was her freedom. Nothing else had mattered and she hadn't wanted any reminders. So she'd left Marty's place with a few personal items and bought some overpriced toiletries at the airport on the way out to Spain. Not a lot to show for ten years.

By the way her mother flinched at the last part of her comment she knew there was an expectation that Inés would stay as long as she was needed. Except she wasn't going to be railroaded. She'd somehow found the strength to leave Marty and his controlling ways and she was determined to break that pattern once and for all.

'I was hoping—'

'Let's just take one day at a time.' She knew exactly what her mother was hoping for, but she wasn't making any promises or commitment. That way if she felt the need to move on, if she couldn't cope being back in this environment, she could move on somewhere else.

For now, she was just happy to have a job and somewhere to stay.

One thing she could be sure of was a steady stream of patients. Despite everything, her father was a good doctor. Plus, being a bilingual practice made them popular with the expat community and tourists who suddenly found themselves in need of medical treatment.

'Hey, Marie, sorry I'm a bit late this morning. The traffic was almost at a standstill.'

A tall figure appeared in the office doorway, taking off a cycle helmet.

Muy guapo!

With a mop of dark unruly hair and deep brown eyes, not to mention the very tight cycling shorts he was wearing leaving very little to the imagination, he was fit in all senses of the word.

How unfortunate that her libido was apparently Spanish and drawn to her fellow country man. Even more unfortunate when she realised who it was.

'Inés, this is Ángelo.' Her mother made the introduction, but judging by his dark glare he had already guessed her identity. It seemed her reputation preceded her. Though she wasn't exactly sure what she'd done to earn his wrath already.

Despite her own misgivings about her new colleague, Inés held out her hand and flashed the biggest smile she could muster. 'It's nice to meet you.'

'I've heard a lot about you,' he responded, pumping her hand once before releasing her. The glower suggesting not everything he'd been told showered her in glory.

It was to be expected, she supposed. According to her father she was the ungrateful daughter who'd shunned the family practice along with her family. Ángelo was the hero who'd swooped in and gratefully taken her place. In her parents' business, as well as their personal lives.

'Likewise,' she said equally coolly and with the same hint of disdain.

'I suppose we should open the doors. Inés is going to start straight away, so it should ease some of the pressure on you, Ángelo.' Efficient as ever, her mother checked her watch. Keen to open the surgery dead on time.

It never ceased to make her wonder how such a strong woman got involved with a controlling man such as her father, who pretty much dictated their life. Then again, Inés had fallen victim to the same kind of toxic relationship. Love made people do stupid things. Exactly why she'd made the decision to forget relationships, focus on work and try to make a life for herself again. Loving meant having to hand over control and she wasn't prepared to do that ever again.

'I'll get changed,' he said, drawing Inés's attention to his taut thighs once more.

She thought it was probably a good idea before he gave some poor patient a heart attack just looking at him.

'Then perhaps you could show Inés how things work around here,' her mother said cheerfully, as though he'd solved all of their problems simply by turning up.

Inés was sure she probably could've figured out the computer system for herself, but she was doing her best to be as amiable as possible and kept her mouth shut.

'Oh, yes, you wouldn't have a clue about how things work around here.' However, Ángelo didn't appear as eager to facilitate a harmonious working environment.

'It's a bit hard to be involved when you live in a different country,' she said through gritted teeth.

Her mother watched the exchange like a spectator at a verbal tennis match, but said nothing. Probably because she wanted to bury her head in the sand as usual and pretend nothing was happening. Though it was pretty clear to Inés already that she and Dr Caballero were not going to get along.

Still, she wasn't going to let that get to her. There was no way she was going to let Ángelo walk all over her. She'd shed two toxic men in her life and she wasn't afraid to stand up for herself any more.

Ángelo changed quickly into his shirt and tie, swapping his shorts for long trousers, so he looked more professional. He hadn't expected to see the prodigal daughter so soon. But here she was and apparently not pleased to see him working here. Tough. He'd been here for her parents when she hadn't and he wasn't going anywhere simply because she'd come back.

This job was his life and he'd worked hard to get here. Once he was sure he was financially stable he hoped to have the family he'd always dreamed about. Until now he hadn't been able to commit to anyone, knowing he couldn't provide a stable home, and he wasn't prepared to settle for anything less. Family was everything to him. Something which his *abuela* had drummed into him after his mother had walked out on him and his brothers, leaving them with their abusive, drunken father.

His grandmother had helped raise them and if it hadn't been for her support they would have starved. After his father lost his job and money was tight, he turned to alcohol, further depleting their income and causing the arguments between his parents. Yet his *abuela* wouldn't hear a bad word about her son, their father. He was family and that was all that mattered. A motto which Ángelo had carried with him and stayed to look after his father when his drinking had caught up with him. Despite his father's violent temper, and his brothers moving out one by one, Ángelo had cared for his father until his death. He didn't want to earn the same bad name his mother had for abandoning her family.

Now he was trying to make a life for himself again and he wasn't going to let a beautiful stranger take that away from him.

Marie and Juan de la Fuente had been good to him. They'd become like a substitute family to him, not only giving him a job, but inviting him into their lives, sharing meals and holidays that he would otherwise have spent alone. He knew Inés was back to help because her father was ill, but for him, that didn't negate the decade she'd apparently spent without giving them a second thought. They were good people and he didn't want to see them get hurt at such a vulnerable time in their lives. He felt very protective over the couple who had taken him in and given him a future to look forward to and he wasn't going to let Inés spoil that.

However, she was another doctor on board and he could use an extra pair of hands to help with the patient list.

Her office door was open, but he knocked anyway.

'Come in.' She glanced up from the desk and her stunning blue eyes swept over him, appearing to give his new work attire her approval. Despite his pre-formed bad opinion of someone who hadn't visited her parents for ten years, he took some pleasure in knowing that she liked what she saw. Even if her appreciative look was fleeting.

24　　　SPANISH DOC TO HEAL HER

'I thought I'd give you a rundown of the software we use here.' It would be churlish of him to leave her to figure out the system for herself, not to mention detrimental to the clinic. He got the feeling she was too stubborn to ask him for help even if she needed it. At least this way he had a clear conscience. Whatever his personal feelings for this woman who'd obviously broken her parents' hearts, they were going to have to work together and continue the clinic's success.

'Thanks.' She kicked back on her swivel chair so she moved away from the computer screen, leaving him some space to lean in and show her the set up.

'This is where you'll find the patient files and this is the appointment system.' It was difficult to concentrate when all he could smell was her floral scent and feel her warm breath on the back of his neck.

He stepped back, putting some much-needed distance between them so he could breathe without filling his lungs with her. It was a distraction he hadn't planned on and wasn't particularly happy about. 'I'm sure you can take it from here.'

'Thanks,' she said curtly.

'We have a few of our frequent fliers as we call them. Patients who come regularly because of their chronic illnesses. I can handle them and I think we've one or two emergency appointments with tourists who might need medical certificates before they're able to fly. Will you be okay to take them?'

She narrowed her eyes at him. 'I'm sure I can manage.'

This new working arrangement was seriously going to test them both and Ángelo knew he wasn't going to be the one to break first. He'd worked too hard to let a virtual stranger walk in and take over. Especially when she didn't have a good track record of sticking around.

CHAPTER TWO

'I'LL JUST CHECK with Dr Caballero and see what the recommended wait is before you can fly back home, Mrs Armitage.' Inés had managed her patient list well so far, with nothing she wasn't used to dealing with in the practice she'd worked at in London.

However, she wasn't completely au fait with the rules and regulations around tourists flying after a medical emergency such as Mrs Armitage's broken arm. She was sure she'd come to learn in time, but for now she was going to have to bite the bullet and consult Ángelo on this one. As the practice manager, her mother had been great at helping her with paperwork, but this was one she was going to need a second opinion on. Unfortunately.

She knocked on his office door.

'Come in. Ah, Inés, how are you getting on?' Alone, he was clearly finishing up his paperwork for the day, but turned to greet her.

She forced herself to appear amicable since she needed his assistance. 'Good. I'm with my last patient of the day now. I just needed your advice, if that's okay?'

'Of course.' He directed her to a seat usually reserved for patients.

'Patient has suffered a broken arm and needs a fit-to-fly letter. I'm just not sure on the timings yet.' She had to swallow her pride and wait for the gloating.

Surprisingly, it didn't come. 'Sure. It's usually recommended that the patient doesn't fly for forty-eight hours after having a plaster cast put on. If they're flying before this, they'll need the cast cut in half to leave room for swelling and expansion at high altitude, to avoid deep vein thrombosis. I've got some info on that sort of thing that might come in handy in the future. We get a lot of tourists needing that kind of advice. Alcohol and sun can lead to a lot of broken bones out here.'

'I'm not sure that's what happened to this particular patient, but thank you.'

Ángelo rummaged in his desk drawer and presented her with a folder. 'Some light reading for you.'

The hefty weight took her two hands to hold. 'I've nothing else to do anyway, so I'll have a look through this tonight. Thanks.'

28   SPANISH DOC TO HEAL HER

'No problem,' he said, turning back to his own work.

Inés couldn't quite figure him out. He'd definitely been put out by her arrival, yet seemed happy to help. Perhaps he was just professional. All she did know was that she needed to be on her guard around him.

Once she'd typed out the letter Mrs Armitage needed to secure her place on a flight home, she began to pack up her things. Including the paperwork Ángelo had given her to swot up for her next tourist emergency.

Her mother appeared in the doorway. 'Are you ready to go?'

'Yes. I can't wait for dinner. I'm starved.' A slight exaggeration since Ángelo had kindly ordered food in for lunch, but she'd worked up an appetite none the less.

It was nice to be back into the swing of working again, not worrying about what she was going home to. Although she was wary about being back in the family home, at least she was safe in the knowledge that her father wasn't there.

'I'm just waiting for Ángelo to put his bike in the back of the car, then we can be on our way.' Her mother dropped the bombshell, then flitted away again to do one last tidy around of the reception area.

Any good feelings she'd been beginning to have towards her co-worker quickly fell away. 'Why is Ángelo coming?'

Her mother stopped cleaning the plastic chairs long enough to frown at her. 'He comes for dinner most nights. Especially since your father got sick. We both enjoy the company.'

'Don't you think that's weird?'

'Don't be silly, Inés. He's a nice boy. Just a bit…lonely, I think. And the house has been very quiet since you left.'

'Well, I'm back now. Doesn't he have any family of his own to have dinner with?' She didn't see the appeal of spending nights with her ageing parents after working with them all day. Unless he was up to something untoward and trying to worm his way in. He certainly seemed to be doing his best to replace her.

Perhaps that was why she was feeling so resentful towards Ángelo, when she hardly knew him. He'd been able to make her parents happy when she'd never managed to do anything other than disappoint them.

She just wished she'd had the support that they seemed to have given Ángelo. Inés had tried her best when it came to studying and trying to please them. But anything less than one hundred per cent was deemed a failure in her father's eyes. His exacting high standards had seemed impossible to meet and it was that feeling of failure which had put her off the idea of joining the family business. Knowing she would never be seen as an equal in the practice. That had been the beginning of her rebellion, of choosing her own path. As far away from her parents' impossible expectations as possible.

She'd needed breathing room, space to figure out who she was and what she wanted. It was ironic that becoming a doctor was what she'd wanted after all, but on her own terms.

Perhaps, if they'd given her that space, she might never have left at all. In fact, far from not wanting a relationship, she found she was envious that Ángelo had slotted easily into the life she was supposed to have had.

Inés felt slightly regretful that things had been left to fester for so long between her and her parents. If they'd all made a better effort to resolve their problems, they could have all benefited from some family support.

'I don't think his parents are still alive, but I think he has a couple of brothers somewhere.'

'Maybe he should have a family reunion of his own then,' Inés muttered.

'Don't be mean. You just need to get to know him better. He's a lovely boy.'

Inés smiled sweetly and resisted correcting

her mother. Ángelo was not a boy, he was most definitely a man.

'I'll have to take your word for that,' she said, following her mother out to her car like a truculent teen.

Ángelo was already there, ensconced in the passenger seat, leaving her to squeeze into the back seat, folding herself in like a pretzel around the bike he'd deposited there.

'Sorry. I'm just so used to jumping in the front lately. Do you want me to swap places with you?' Ángelo began to unbuckle his seatbelt.

'It's okay. I wouldn't want to put you to any trouble.' Inés caught his gaze in the rearview mirror and batted her eyelashes which were more real than her smile.

Ángelo and her mother made small talk the whole way back to the house. Leaving Inés feeling like an outsider. Just as she had at school and later when she'd moved to England. Not part of any little cliques and very much isolated. That ingrained need to study and be the best had travelled with her to England. It seemed even away from her father's influence, that work ethic remained and her focus had been on becoming a doctor. She'd seen the difference her father had made in people's everyday lives and she'd been drawn to general practice. Something familiar in her new world.

With little money, and no family around her for support, she'd worked odd jobs where she could and shared student accommodation until graduation. Even as a junior doctor, she'd shared a house with several colleagues, though the long working hours and conflicting shifts meant she'd never really got close to anyone. Relationships had been scarce and brief. Not everyone shared her work, eat, sleep, repeat, routine. And drinking and partying with every other twenty-somethings would have distracted her from her ultimate goal of becoming the kind of doctor her parents should have been proud of. As a result, she'd become a bit of a loner. Albeit a great doctor.

That self-imposed isolation was probably what had made her an easy target for a man like Marty. A mature, successful surgeon, who'd shown a considerable interest in her in the time they'd both worked in the same hospital, had been hard for her to resist. In hindsight, perhaps she'd been looking for the approval of an older man because of her difficult relationship with her family. Marty had certainly given her that. At first.

To get her to go out with him, he'd love bombed her with gifts and kind words. Flattered and craving that connection with someone who seemed to appreciate her, she'd been easily won over. Expensive restaurants, luxury weekend breaks away and an incredibly romantic partner made falling for him inevitable. After that, things had moved quickly and it wasn't long before they'd begun living together in his apartment.

Given her family circumstances, Marty hadn't had to worry about friends or family getting involved in their personal business and he'd kept it that way. Quickly becoming her world. She hadn't noticed his subtle manipulation at first. He'd had a way of making her feel as though she was on a pedestal at times, so she'd ignored any little niggles. Like convincing her that things needed to be done his way for it to be right. Cooking, cleaning, even what she wore, all had to be to his requirements. Subtly taking away her autonomy until she questioned every decision she made outside of work. Gaslighting her into believing she wasn't capable of doing anything for herself.

It was a wonder he'd let her keep working, though she supposed that was so that she kept bringing an income into the house. Which, of course, he took control of, too, telling her that he was happy to deal with the financial matters of the household. Taking the burden of worrying about bills away from her. Her wages going straight into his account, inevitably making it harder for her to break free.

It was an even bigger mystery how she, a very competent GP, could be so easily led in her personal life. Though she supposed her childhood, dominated by a similar character, made it easier for her to continue that pattern. Especially when Marty kept telling her her parents couldn't have loved her to treat her the way they had. Encouraging her to keep her distance when her mother had occasionally reached out to her, telling her he was the only person she needed in her life. That he was the only one who truly loved her. Stealing away any chance to ever repair her relationship with her family. One more thing he took away from her.

In the end, it was talk of marriage and children which finally woke her up to the reality of her situation. She'd treated a patient who'd obviously been very badly beaten by her partner, but she'd insisted on covering for him, saying her injuries had been her own fault and refusing to point the finger at her scowling husband hovering nearby. Regardless that there were young children in the household who clearly needed protecting, too.

When Marty had told her it was time they started a family, she knew that level of commitment would have meant being trapped in the relationship for ever. No doubt he would have got her to stop working, going out in public altogether, once he knew she was officially his. Then there were the children...

The anxious faces of her patient's young offspring had haunted her. She didn't want to inflict that restrictive upbringing she'd endured on to another generation. Certainly not with a man whose temper had a tendency to flare up at the smallest perceived inconvenience. Someone she couldn't be one hundred per cent sure wouldn't put her in the same position as the woman she'd treated.

She'd waited until he'd gone to work, packed her bags and moved out. Telling him in a voice message she wasn't coming back and spending the next weeks dodging his calls, and ranting messages. Until her mother had got in touch and offered her a way out from it all.

She shuddered at the thought of her lucky escape. The reception she'd received from her mother made her wonder if Marty had simply fed into her teenage sense of injustice which had taken her to England. Perhaps if he'd let her work through her issues without adding to that feeling that her parents didn't love her, she might have seen her actions, and theirs, with a different level of maturity and understanding. That guilt and shame that she'd been manipulated into severing

SPANISH DOC TO HEAL HER

ties with her family until it was too late, making her question if she even deserved their love and support now. She'd left them to deal with her father's illness alone and she should be grateful they'd had Ángelo here.

Inés hoped being back in Spain was going to make a difference to everyone. Not only was she getting to know her mother again, but she had free will for the first time in years. She was earning her own money and could leave any time she chose. Putting up with Ángelo was a small price to pay.

Once they had arrived at the villa, Inés left him to wrangle the bike back out of the car and walked on inside behind her mother. She hadn't really taken time to look around when she'd arrived, but now she could see nothing had really changed here. It was both comforting and haunting. Familiar, yet frightening. Good and bad memories so inextricably linked to these surroundings.

As the automatic gates closed behind them, she was reminded of how isolated the property was. The outside locked away from sight. It was a beautiful villa and her parents had worked hard for it, but she'd felt trapped here. She took a stroll around the small pool which had been her one source of freedom. Even if her father had curtailed the time she spent there and made sure she washed down the area around it every time she used it.

The blue tiles at the bottom of the water glinted in the sun, teasing her and making her want to jump in for old times' sake. She hadn't gone swimming since leaving Spain and she wondered if anyone still used the pool. It was clean and well maintained and the floral-cushioned sun loungers were still dotted around for those who preferred sun worshipping. No doubt Ángelo made use of the place as he seemed to be everywhere else.

'It's a lovely garden. Sometimes your father would barbecue out here, but I suppose you know all of that.' Ángelo sounded behind her and she fought hard not to roll her eyes.

'I can't say he ever barbecued anything for me. It would have caused too much mess and smoke. At least, that's what he used to tell me. But I guess people change.' She just wasn't sure how much. It made her think about what she had missed in the intervening years. If her father had mellowed, if he'd been remorseful about what had happened between them. It made it even more sad that they hadn't resolved their differences earlier.

Inés turned and walked into the villa, the cool tiles and neutral colours so abundant in Spanish properties, a world away from her centrally heated flat with plush carpets and vibrant decor. Though she supposed that wasn't hers any more either. Not that it ever had been. Marty had always made sure to remind her it was his flat and he was simply letting her stay. So she lived in constant fear that he could kick her out at any moment if she upset him. Ironic when he'd made it so hard for her to leave.

Being back now felt very much like when she'd first left home, with nothing to her name. Except those ten years she'd spent working and building a life now seemed a waste of time and effort.

She went to her old room to deposit her bag. It hadn't changed either. Her old black and white arty prints still hanging on the wall and the same crocheted cover on the bed which she'd spent many nights crying her frustration into.

A smile played on her lips as she lifted her old jewellery box from the top of her dresser. Upon opening, the ballerina inside spun around on one wonky foot as the music played. She poked her finger into the contents, uncovering the treasures of her teenage years. A badge she'd won in a school quiz, plastic pink hoop earrings she bought herself the first, and only, time she went shopping with school mates—her father quickly put a stop to that. He didn't like her wasting money on petty trinkets, nor hanging around with people who were a bad influence on her. She trailed her finger over the tiny gold cross pendant she had got for her eighteenth birthday.

Not that she'd been allowed a big party like all of her peers to celebrate her birthday. Her father had insisted they simply had one at home. A regular dinner with a small birthday cake for dessert. She'd been crushed, wanting to dress up and party like every other eighteen-year-old. But Father had insisted she didn't need any of that to mark her adulthood. No, she just needed to work at the family practice. So began his plans for her to move into the family business, marking out her future for her without letting her have any say.

She closed the lid on the jewellery box. Everything in the house was tainted by her father's need for control.

Now he was fighting for his own life, his presence noticeably absent in the home she'd come to despise, she wasn't sure how to feel. She didn't wish him to suffer, but when it came to any feelings deeper than sympathy for his plight, she was just kind of...numb. That could change, of course, depending on what happened next, but her emotions were currently adrift. Out of her reach. And she wasn't sure she really wanted to

40 SPANISH DOC TO HEAL HER

catch up with them in the near future when she'd already been through so much.

Walking back into the kitchen didn't help improve her mood.

'What way do you want these peppers sliced, Marie?' Ángelo asked, ensconced at the kitchen worktop, apron covering his work clothes.

'Just dice them, please, Ángelo.' Her mother was in her element at the hob, stirring pots and setting out dishes. A cosy domestic scene which made her feel ill.

'Anything I can do?' If this hadn't been the cuckoo in her parents' nest, she might have been impressed by a man helping to prepare dinner. Goodness knew neither her father, nor Marty, had ever lifted a finger in the kitchen. Only complained when the food hadn't been quite right, or things weren't as spotless as they'd wanted.

Ángelo seemed comfortable in his role as sous chef. As though it was something he often did. Her mother certainly seemed happy with the arrangement. It made her yearn for the chance to have the same ease with her parents. Made her question how he'd achieved it when she hadn't. If she simply hadn't been good enough for them as she'd always suspected. And if there was any chance of ever having this sort of relationship with them given the circumstances of her father's health and the fact that Ángelo had been here for them when she hadn't.

'Sit. Sit. Ángelo and I have everything in hand.' Her mother dismissed her offer of help with a wave of her hand and carried on cooking. Making Inés feel as though she was a visitor, not an actual member of the family.

'What's on the menu?' She did her best to try to be included. If she was staying here for the foreseeable future and this was an ongoing arrangement, she was going to have to get used to the way they did things. Or somehow find a way to be a part of it.

'Just some tapas. It's quick and easy after a day at work.' Inés's mother began dishing out the food and Ángelo retrieved a bottle of white wine from the fridge.

Inés supposed having company at home stopped her mother dwelling too much on what was happening with her father. She knew what it was to feel alone in the world, lost and frightened. No doubt everything her mother was feeling right now.

'It's nice tonight. Why don't we take this outside?' Without waiting for a response, Ángelo headed out towards the patio, leaving Inés and her mother to carry the earthenware tapas dishes out to the table.

He ducked back inside to grab some wine

glasses and cutlery and they made a makeshift dinner table in the garden. Inés had to admit it was nice to be able to sit outside at this time of the evening, feeling the heat of the sun on her skin. If it wasn't for her terminally ill father, her broken relationship with her parents and a stranger suddenly immersed in her life, this might've felt like a holiday. Certainly the closest she'd come to one in ten years.

Marty had been a workaholic and expected her to be the same. If she had had any free time, he always found something to keep her busy. At the beginning of the relationship she'd been happy to do the housework, to look after her man. It had made her feel as though she had created a life away from Spain when she was responsible for running her own house. After a while it became obvious that Marty thought that all domestic chores were her department, regardless that she had a career, too. He wanted a little woman at home to look after him, and in retrospect, he didn't do anything for her in return.

There was no divvying up of jobs. He didn't take out the bins or dry the dishes. He simply expected her to take care of it all and if she didn't do it, or things weren't done to his standard, then she'd never hear the end of it. It had been easier simply to do everything rather than listen to him lecture her about the 'traditional' role he expected her to fulfil in his life. No doubt taking over from the mother who had pandered to her only son's every whim and made him into the little emperor he'd become. In hindsight, it hadn't been only her father's footsteps she'd followed in, but her mother's, too.

Inés took a sip of wine, closed her eyes, and let the sun caress her skin. Yes, this was a taste of the freedom she'd been searching for. It was ironic she'd found it at the place she'd run from a decade ago.

'You look as though you need some sun,' her mother said with a tut, forcing her to open her eyes.

'And more wine.' Ángelo reached across the table to top up her glass.

'Perhaps you should have taken a day or two to settle in before you started work.' Her mother was staring at her with a frown and Inés worried she could see right into her soul and everything she'd been dealing with prior to flying out.

When she'd asked Inés if it was possible she could fill in for her father at the clinic for a while, she'd agreed, saying she needed a change and wanted to help. She hadn't mentioned Marty, a break up, or anything which would've caused worry or curiosity.

The same reason she wouldn't admit to being tired now.

44   SPANISH DOC TO HEAL HER

Inés didn't want sympathy, pity or criticism for getting into such a toxic relationship and staying so long. She especially didn't want it from Mr Perfect who couldn't seem to do any wrong. Who seemed to have his life completely together and was making her irrationally jealous because she'd failed at doing just that.

'I'm fine. Just soaking up some much-needed vitamin D,' she assured them.

'How did you get on today?' Her mother began cutting into the tortilla, the smell of which was making Inés's mouth water.

It was a long time since she'd had home cooking, or any decent Spanish food. She'd become accustomed to British stodgy comfort food, but in the sun it was good to have something so familiar.

'Good. I need to brush up on the tourist side of things, but Ángelo gave me some info to read on that.' She helped herself to a slice of the potato and egg omelette which her mother had flavoured with peppers and onion.

'It won't be long until you're in the swing of things.' Ángelo passed her the other dishes and she added chunks of jamon and cheese, and some anchovies, to her plate.

Inés knew from experience that, even though these little dishes didn't look like much on their own, they were deceptively filling. It was a good way to end the day with a drink in company and a full belly. Even if that company was another man she had reason to be wary of. At least Marty and her father had taught her not to be taken in by a handsome face and a charm offensive.

A companionable silence fell between the trio as they ate and drank, winding down after the day. It was her mother who broke the spell and reminded her why she was really here.

'So...how long do you think you'll be here for, Inés?'

'I don't really know. Why? Do you need the room back?' She was attempting humour, but going by Ángelo's judgy look she'd fallen flat.

Her mother, too, looked aghast. 'No. Of course not. You know you're welcome to stay here as long as you want. You always have been.'

Now she felt bad and the omelette her mother had lovingly prepared now weighed heavily in her stomach. 'I know. I don't want to get into all of that now.'

She stared pointedly at Ángelo in the hope her mother would get the hint that she didn't want to discuss their personal business in front of him. Her parents might be comfortable around him, but she hardly knew him and had no desire to change that either.

'I think your mother just wants to know you're not going to disappear again, when this is already a very trying time for her.' Ángelo's sudden, and unwarranted, contribution to the conversation left Inés seething.

Clearly, he'd been told something of her past and her estrangement from her parents. Not enough, however, to realise that he was out of order and had no idea what he was talking about.

'It's a very difficult time for all of us. I'm an adult and if, and when, I'm ready to leave I'll discuss it with you, Mama. We both know there were reasons why I left, but I'm willing to set those aside for now to help out. I'm here for you and the practice.' Not Ángelo. Her personal life was not his business and she didn't owe him anything. Certainly not an explanation, or her schedule.

'I'm sure Ángelo didn't mean anything, Inés. We're grateful that you're here. For however long we have you. I'm sure your father will be content knowing the practice is in safe hands.' Her mother was doing her best to keep the peace as she always had. Though it had always seemed a cop out to Inés, never fully supporting her daughter. Even now she was defending Ángelo's attitude.

She took a deep breath and reminded herself she had nowhere else to go, so she'd have to simply hold her tongue. And her temper.

'Actually, I think today has caught up with

me. I'm going to have an early night. Leave the dishes and I'll do them in the morning.' She feigned a yawn and excused herself from the table before anyone had the chance to say goodnight.

Tomorrow she'd be better prepared for Ángelo's jibes. She might even tell him exactly why she'd left and knock her parents off the pedestal he seemed to have placed them on, once and for ever.

'I'm sorry. I didn't mean to upset Inés.' Despite their clash of personalities, Ángelo hadn't intended to bring the evening to such an abrupt end.

He couldn't seem to help himself looking out for Marie and Juan when they'd been so good to him. From what he'd seen and heard, they'd been hurt by their daughter's departure ten years ago. More so by her reluctance to maintain any sort of relationship. He hated to think of them going through that pain again. Especially given Juan's health at present.

However, he had to remember that Juan was Inés's father. She'd come back to help and she did deserve his compassion. Regardless that they seemed to rub each other up the other way. Something they would have to get over when they were going to be working together for the foreseeable future.

Ángelo resolved to apologise. Tomorrow. After she'd cooled off, and he'd given her some space from his bout of foot in mouth. Clearly something had gone on in the family which he hadn't been privy to. And as close as he was, he wasn't part of it. It was no wonder Inés seemed to resent his presence. He'd got too comfortable, but her sudden reappearance had reminded them both that these were her parents, not his. His were long gone and had never been as supportive as Marie and Juan.

'She'll be all right. My daughter has always had a bit of a temper. That's why she and Juan used to clash. Too much like one another,' Marie sighed, finishing her glass of wine.

'She's entitled to feel how she feels when a stranger interferes in her personal life. It's none of my business and I shouldn't have commented at all. I'll apologise tomorrow.' He didn't like the idea of dismissing how she felt. How he'd made her feel.

Growing up with violence, physical and emotional abuse, he knew what it was like to have your feelings dismissed. He would never forgive himself for hurting anyone. When his mother had left him and his brothers when he was only seven years old, his father had beaten him for crying. Told him to man up. The same sentiment coming from his *abuela* who'd told him his mother wasn't worth his tears since she'd abandoned her family. Something which was all important to her. It had been his *abuela's* influence which had driven him to stay with his abusive father long after the rest of the family had moved out, looking after his only parent until he passed away.

Angelo knew he was the one in the wrong here and, given that Inés hadn't bitten back as she had earlier in the clinic, he knew he'd hurt her. A matter he hoped to make amends for—perhaps they could call a truce to make things easier for them at work. He knew what a toxic environment felt like and didn't want to be responsible for cultivating one now. They both wanted to make the practice a success in her father's absence.

As far as he could tell, both of their futures depended on it. Although she hadn't mentioned a life away from here, he got the impression she'd left the one she'd had in London for good. Only time would tell if she intended to stay here for any length of time, but for now she didn't seem to have any other place to go when she'd avoided her parents up until now.

'I should probably get home too.' He finished the last crumbs of jamon and cheese, washing them down with the rest of his wine. Glad he only had a short bike ride home.

'Thanks for your help tonight, Ángelo.' Marie got up to see him out. 'And please, don't let Inés get under your skin.'

All he could do was offer a weak smile in response because he had a feeling she already had.

CHAPTER THREE

INÉS TOOK HER stethoscope off after sounding her patient's heart and finding nothing out of the ordinary which would be causing her sudden fatigue. 'I think we should run some blood tests and make sure there's not something more going on other than running after two small children, Mrs Ramirez.'

She let the young woman rebutton her blouse and began ordering the tests she wanted run. Her mother, as well as being the practice manager, had taken a phlebotomy course and was qualified to take the bloods for her. No doubt a cost-effective initiative her father had implemented in Inés's absence, but she was proud her mother had added to her skill set over the years.

'Do I need to worry?' A frown furrowed Mrs Ramirez's forehead, but Inés didn't like to pre-empt a diagnosis until she had all of the facts at hand.

'Your heart sounds perfectly fine and I haven't seen anything to give me great concern. However, I want to investigate a bit more. Any headaches? Nausea?' She printed off some patient labels and added them to the vials for her mother to fill and send off to the lab for analysis this afternoon before she left. With her father nearing his last days, her mother spent as much time as she could by his side and did her best to complete her work early in the day. They had a temp in as and when she was needed, with an unwritten agreement that she would be filling in full time at some point.

'I have been feeling a bit off colour, but I just put that down to lack of sleep.' Although it wasn't unheard of for new mums to be exhausted, there was something about Mrs Ramirez's pale complexion which was making Inés think there might be more to it.

'Okay, we'll get these bloods done and I'll call you back in for another appointment. We'll take it from there.' Inés got up to see her out and pass on the details of the tests she wanted to her mother.

Mrs Ramirez stood to leave, then reached out to grip the corner of the desk, suddenly swaying.

'Mrs Ramirez?' Inés reached out too late as the woman's eyes appeared to roll back in her head and she collapsed on the floor.

Inés rushed to her side immediately and tried

to rouse her. 'Elena? Can you hear me? Open your eyes for me.'

She checked the woman's pulse—it was faint and her breathing laboured. Inés immediately moved her into the recovery position and ran to the door.

'Ángelo? I need help in here!' she yelled so he would hear her through his closed door, not wanting to leave her patient.

Immediately, he and her mother came running to see what was wrong.

'Mama, can you call for an ambulance? Mrs Ramirez was complaining of fatigue, got up to leave and just passed out. I think she hit her head on the desk on her way down.' Guilt weighed heavily on her shoulders that she hadn't been able to catch her patient before she sustained the injury. Especially now that a pool of blood was gradually staining the floor scarlet.

Her mother hurried off to call for help and Ángelo immediately got down on the floor beside Mrs Ramirez, with Inés taking position on the other side of her.

'Mrs Ramirez? It's Dr Caballero. Can you hear me?' The woman remained unresponsive.

'I don't like that tinge to her lips.' Inés noticed the sudden blue appearance, the cyanosis possibly indicating low oxygen content in the blood.

54   SPANISH DOC TO HEAL HER

She checked Mrs Ramirez's pulse, listened to her heart and realised she'd gone into cardiac arrest.

When she told Ángelo, he immediately ran out of the room and grabbed the defibrillator off the wall in the reception area. Inés set to work opening the woman's blouse so they had access to her chest and began CPR, only stopping briefly once Ángelo had placed the sticky pads on to the woman's torso and the robotic voice of the defibrillator told her to stop chest compressions in order for the machine to analyse the heart's rhythm.

'Stand clear.' Ángelo issued the instruction they'd both been taught when using a defibrillator to make sure no one was touching the patient.

'Shock advised. Charging. Stand clear,' the machine instructed and both doctors had to wait until it told them they could push the shock button to deliver the first shock.

Once Ángelo pressed the red button and the machine had done its job, it was Inés's turn and she restarted CPR. After a couple of minutes, the machine re-analysed and suggested a second shock. Sometimes one shock was all that was needed to bring someone back to responsive and breathing, but not in this case. Inés started chest compressions again, with Ángelo watching their patient for a response.

'Wait. I think we've got her back.' He put a

hand out to stop Inés and put his head down to listen for signs of life.

Inés checked the woman's pulse. It was faint, but it was there. 'Thank goodness.'

She hadn't realised she'd voiced her relief aloud and wondered if it would make her seem unprofessional when Ángelo seemed so calm about the event. He made no comment as they moved Mrs Ramirez into the recovery position and they were able to finally sit back and breathe.

The paramedics rushed in and Inés gave them her patient's details, along with a debrief of their resuscitation efforts. It was a scenario she'd been part of a few times, but it was the first time in years that she'd felt as though she had any support. Marty had kept her so isolated, so afraid to reach out to anyone and incur his wrath, she'd all but distanced everyone she worked with up until now.

By the time the paramedics were wheeling Mrs Ramirez out to the ambulance, Ángelo had disappeared. It left Inés a little deflated after all of the drama to suddenly find herself on her own again. She flopped down in the chair at her desk. This was the part she missed about being in a relationship. Not having anyone to discuss her day with and process what had happened.

Though it was a small price to pay for her freedom, she supposed.

There was a knock on her office door.

'Come in.' She was surprised to see Ángelo appear carrying a tray of coffees and pastries.

'I thought you might need this.' He unloaded the coffees on to her desk and sat in the patient chair to join her.

Up until their last encounter she would rather have boiled her own head in the coffee maker than sit with him, but she needed the company right now.

'Thanks.' She accepted his offering in the nature it had been intended. Graciously.

With adrenalin still pumping through her body, she wasn't sure she needed the caffeine hit, but she did need time to process what had happened. Work her way through events in her head and reassure herself she'd done everything she could. Although they'd brought Mrs Ramirez back, Inés would replay the drama on a loop as she always did until she was sure the woman was going to be okay.

'I just wanted to make sure you were okay. That was a crazy afternoon.' Ángelo passed her one of the little pastries, fitting a whole one into his mouth. He had quite the appetite from what she'd seen so far. It was remarkable how slim he was considering, but she supposed the cycling helped him burn off the calories. She would have to take up swimming again if she continued to eat so well. Marty had always watched what she ate, ready to criticise if he thought she'd gained as much as a pound. For her own health, he'd told her. But, like everything in hindsight, she could see now it was just another way of controlling her.

Following Ángelo's lead, she wolfed down the sweet treat, enjoying it guilt free for once.

'Yes. Thanks for your help.'

'I think you were doing fine on your own, but we're a team here. We have to work together.' He offered her a warming smile which eroded some of those defences she'd recently built to defend herself. She couldn't take another man riding in and trying to take control her life again.

'I know. I think I've got used to doing things on my own, but I appreciate the back up.' If it had been Marty assisting her, he would have criticised everything she'd done. Probably taken over completely, then spent this debrief telling her how she should have done things, completely undermining her confidence, and making her believe she couldn't do her job properly. As her superior when she'd worked in the hospital, he'd double-checked her every diagnosis and treatment. And she'd accepted that intimation that she couldn't be trusted to get things right, even when she had an exemplary record, because she'd been so used to her father's criticism.

However, Marty had continued to undermine her even when it came to their personal relationship. He'd made her start doubting herself and in the end it had been proved she couldn't trust her own judgement. Otherwise she would never have ended up living with a replica of her father.

She shuddered, knowing how close she'd come to being trapped in that toxic relationship permanently. With no job, no income, there would have been no escape.

Although she was living back home for now, she still had free will and some money coming in. As far as she could tell Ángelo didn't present a threat to any of that. Perhaps she should give him the benefit of the doubt that they'd simply got off on the wrong foot and there wasn't any more to it than that. It would be nice simply to get on with life without living in that constant fear that someone was trying to hurt her.

Ángelo cleared his throat as though he was about to say something, then took a sip of coffee, delaying the moment. As though the words were sticking in his craw.

'About last night… I was out of order. I shouldn't have said anything about your relationship with your parents. It's none of my business.'

Inés could tell it had taken a lot for him to

say that. He was clearly very protective of her parents, which was odd in itself, but he wasn't too proud to apologise. A novelty for her. She couldn't remember the last time a man in her life had said sorry for anything. People like her father, and Marty, usually saw it as a sign of weakness. Since Ángelo was making an effort to thaw working relations between them, she thought she should, too. Especially when they had been able to work so well together as a team in an emergency. It would make life easier here at least, even if things at home were tricky.

'It's not, but I think my parents have given you only half of the story.'

Ángelo shook his head. 'It's between you and your parents. I had no business interfering.'

No, he didn't, but she didn't want to go on working here with him thinking the worst of her.

'I can tell you and my father get on well, but he was a very different man when I was growing up.'

Ángelo shifted uncomfortably in his seat as though he didn't want to hear any more which might tarnish the image of the man he seemed to know.

Inés continued regardless. 'I'm sure you've seen for yourself that he runs the show here. He's in charge. Mama falls into line. Well, he expected that at home, too. From both of us. He was controlling. To the point of suffocation.'

She thought she saw a flash of something in Ángelo's eyes. His jaw tightened and his lips drew into a thin line. She was saying things he likely didn't want to hear, but she was done being seen as the bad, ungrateful daughter. If they were going to have any kind of working relationship, she needed him to understand why she'd been away for so long. Even if she didn't tell him the personal circumstances which had forced her back.

If she hadn't been going through such a rough time in her relationship with Marty and needing a way out, she couldn't be one hundred per cent sure she would have returned, regardless of her father's health, or her mother's pleas. She liked to think that perhaps she would have felt enough compassion, but after everything that had happened growing up she simply couldn't be certain.

Her parents hadn't shown her much consideration growing up. They'd only seemed to care about what they wanted. So her feelings, her plans, weren't deemed important. Making that break so she could have some control in her life again had seemed so final, for her own sake. Now, she wondered if she'd just needed a little space. If it hadn't been for Marty's interference, perhaps she might have salvaged her relationship with her family sooner.

'I know he's very single minded, stubborn even. I suppose that's how he made such a success of his practice.' Ángelo was diplomatic in his response, not denying her truth, but making his own observations.

Still, Inés wanted to say her piece just this once, then she'd hopefully never have to explain herself to him, or anybody else, again. 'It's also why we were never allowed to run our own lives. He had to control us too. Make sure everything was up to his standard, whether it was telling my mother how to run the house properly, or forcing his daughter to study even in the school holidays. It didn't earn me many friends. Which he preferred. He saw a teenage girl's social life as a distraction, unimportant. I may have disagreed.'

She attempted some levity, only drawing a nod of Ángelo's head in response. There didn't seem any point in going into the details of the arguments and punishments resulting from that difference of opinion. It wasn't the only thing they'd clashed on. Where her mother had decided it was easier to simply go along with her father's wishes and play the subservient role, Inés had tried to make her voice known. To no avail. In the end, she was the child, he was the adult and she'd had to capitulate. At least until she became of age and had the means to leave.

'I'm sure it wasn't an easy time. Although I didn't know him back then, I do think your father has mellowed over the years. Perhaps he regretted his actions?' Ángelo was trying his best to put a spin on the matter, but Inés still bore the psychological scars from her father's behaviour and, even if he had changed, she wasn't sure she could forgive him. If she hadn't have grown up in that very toxic, controlling environment, there was every chance she wouldn't have ended up with someone like Marty. There might have been a chance for her to be happy.

'Well, if he does, he's never expressed it.'

'Perhaps he would if you visited him…'

Inés narrowed her eyes at him. So much for not interfering in business that wasn't his.

Ángelo held his hands up. 'It's merely a suggestion. It would give you both closure before it's too late. Family is family, no matter what.'

Inés couldn't bring herself to believe that. There might not be anything she could do about who her family was, but that didn't mean she had to put up with it. She supposed that's what had formed this unease between her and Ángelo from the start if he was loyal to a fault.

'Sometimes you have to do what's right for

you. No matter how selfish that might seem to outsiders.'

Ángelo didn't argue or agree, but she got the impression this was a subject they would never see eye to eye on. Nor did they have to, as long as they respected one another's opinion. It wasn't as though she was going to be here for ever anyway.

Ángelo understood her stance, even if he didn't agree with it. It was the same attitude his brothers had taken once they were old enough to leave home. Family didn't appear to mean anything when they couldn't even be bothered to stay in touch with him. Regardless that he'd looked after their father right until his dying day. Putting up with the verbal and physical abuse even into adulthood, even though it went unappreciated.

Even his mother, whom he'd tried to reach out to, had been more interested in the new life she'd made for herself away from her family and hadn't seemed all that interested in getting to know him again. It had been hard to take when he'd been willing to forgive her, but she'd eventually severed all contact.

He'd heard later that she'd passed away and he'd grieved for the woman he'd barely known, along with the mother/son relationship which had never recovered. Still, he had a clear conscience because he knew he'd tried and he wasn't sure he could say the same for his brothers. Perhaps that was part of the reason he was so keen for Inés to make amends with her father, so she didn't have any regrets later in life either.

Inés seemed conflicted about her own family and little wonder. He could see why she was resentful of her father if he had been so unyielding in her youth, but the fact that she was back, helping out, suggested all wasn't lost. Though, in future, he knew now it was a subject he would do better to tiptoe around. Clearly he didn't know all of the details and she was still hurting from whatever had happened between her and her parents in the past.

It made him think of his brothers and their shared childhood. Perhaps those painful memories had prevented them from staying in touch, too, if they were keen to put it all behind them. Both circumstances made him sad for the families which had been torn apart by bad feeling, and difficult upbringings. More than anything he wanted the kind of family around him that his *abuela* had tried to convince him he could have. Made him believe that if he stayed with his father through thick and thin, that he'd love him back. Show him some of the affection he'd so desperately craved. Now all he could do was hope some day he'd find that with a family of his own.

He'd thought he'd found that with Camila, his ex. Only to find he wasn't enough to keep her happy either. Money causing problems again when she didn't think he could provide her with the kind of lifestyle she wanted. Since she'd left him, he'd been too guarded to get into another committed relationship. He'd kept things casual, only prepared to get involved in a serious relationship once he knew he was financially stable. So his family wouldn't be torn apart by the same problems he'd endured growing up.

The first step had been taking this job at Juan's practice. With Inés here, working as hard as he was, he hoped that his position was safe for a while.

'Well, I know both of your parents are glad to have you here. As am I.' It was true.

More and more he'd felt as though he was holding things together here with Juan's health in rapid decline. Although he wasn't afraid of hard work, and hoped to one day run a practice of his own, it was good to have someone else here putting in the hours. He and Inés might have had their differences, but when it had come down to it, they'd been able to work together to save a patient's life. He couldn't ask for much more. Except perhaps for a guarantee she'd be

66 SPANISH DOC TO HEAL HER

staying on a more permanent arrangement. He was beginning to enjoy having her around and that probably wasn't a good idea when she didn't seem to have a long-term plan for being here.

If he'd gone on first appearances, he never would've thought this beautiful, smart, sassy lady would have asked him for help in any circumstances. The first thing she'd done when Mrs Ramirez had collapsed had been to shout for assistance. That wasn't a sign of weakness. It was the mark of a good doctor who put the welfare of her patient first instead of her feelings. He'd worked with a lot of people over the years whose ego wouldn't let them ask for help, much to the detriment of those they'd been treating. Inés was exactly the kind of person he wanted working beside him in a medical emergency.

'I hope so,' she said with a sad sort of half-smile, as though she didn't quite believe him.

Ángelo could see she was wary and even had some inkling now as to why she'd been so defensive since her arrival. Clearly, she and her parents had parted acrimoniously and it was natural that she would hesitate to get close to them again. After all, whatever had happened between them had caused her to leave the country to get away from them. The fact that she was here meant that she hadn't slammed the door completely shut on her relationship with her family. Ángelo hoped for all of their sakes that they could find some peace before Juan passed away. Only time would tell what would happen after that.

Inés had shared some very personal information with him, blunting some of the spikiness she'd used so far to defend herself. Although Ángelo appreciated that she was trying to forge some sort of bond to better their working relationship, he wasn't ready to open up the same way. He wasn't sure he ever would be.

He preferred to keep what had happened during his childhood private. Other than his brothers, no one else knew about that time in his life now his father and grandmother had passed away. If anyone ever had reason to run away from home, it had likely been him, but he hadn't. He'd stayed and been a good son to his abusive father until the very end.

It wasn't a story he intended to use to garner sympathy, or, indeed, criticism for staying too long in that terrible environment. Nor to justify where he was in his life today—single and without a family until he could afford to sufficiently provide for one. It was simply his life and was no one else's business but his. Part of the reason he'd realised why he needed to back off from interfering in Inés's personal life. He certainly wouldn't have appreciated the same in return. Going forward, they both needed to keep their private lives separate from their work. Then he wouldn't be open to having her tell him how he should be living his life either.

'I think we both got off on the wrong foot, but I appreciate you being here, Inés. I'm hoping we can start over, because I'm really looking forward to working with you.' He held out his hand, hoping she would agree to wipe the slate clean.

Having a young, compassionate doctor would bring a whole new dynamic to the practice. As Inés shook his hand he saw her really smile for the first time since she'd arrived. Those stunning blue eyes sparkled and something he saw there seemed to squeeze his heart, stop the breath leaving his lungs. He'd witnessed a glimpse of the person behind the tough exterior she'd built around herself.

A sensitive woman who'd been hurt and who was afraid of letting anyone close again. He recognised the pain and wondered if that was the reason he'd been so resistant to her in the first place. Despite everything, he admired her spirit and they had a lot in common. Damn it, he liked her. And more than anything, he was worried it was going to get in the way of everything he'd been working towards.

Perhaps it would have been safer to remain on opposing sides of the battlefield instead.

CHAPTER FOUR

INÉS HAD DECLINED her mother's offer of a lift to work, having decided to walk and enjoy the cooler morning temperatures before the heat became stifling. She was still trying to get used to permanent sunshine after enduring ten years of murky British weather.

'I'm trying to be strong, Ángelo, but he's just not the man he was.'

Inés walked in just in time to see her mother breaking down in tears, her presence unnoticed as Ángelo gathered her weeping parent into his arms.

'I know, Marie, but he has you. And you have me and Inés. We'll get through this.' He gave her mother a hug and met Inés's eyes.

She mouthed a thank you and he responded with a tip of his head towards her. It was good of him to give her mother the comfort Inés couldn't quite bring herself to give yet. He was compassionate, more than she'd ever seen in her father.

Something invaluable to her mother as well as his patients, she imagined.

She supposed she should be grateful he'd been here for her parents through all of this when she hadn't been able to. Apart from her emotional issues where her parents were concerned, Marty would never have let her take off to a foreign country without him for an unspecified amount of time. Regardless of the fact her father was dying, he wouldn't have let her have that kind of freedom from his influence. Marty wanted to be her whole world. So she didn't want, or need, anything or anyone else. Making her totally reliant on him.

Looking back, she wondered if part of the reason she'd been estranged from her parents for so long had been because of Marty, too. He'd encouraged the separation, told her she didn't need them in her life. Which meant he'd been able to isolate her even more. Have more control over her.

It made her angry to think that she had been so easily manipulated. She needed this time and space to think properly and decide for herself what she wanted, who or what she didn't need in her life. Marty was at the top of that list.

She walked on through to her office, affording her mother and Ángelo some privacy. Feeling as though she'd intruded, even though it was her family. It wasn't that she didn't feel anything towards her parents, but she was conflicted. And wary. She didn't want to jump feet first into the situation, her emotions firmly wrapped up in the moment, only to leave herself vulnerable. First, she needed to work through those emotions for herself. Without any outside interference.

As if on cue, Ángelo appeared in the doorway of her office. 'Sorry if that was a little awkward. Your mother was upset about your father.'

'Has something happened?' The blood seemed to freeze in her veins at the thought her father's condition must have worsened for her mother to have been so upset.

Despite the circumstances, it was difficult for her to support either of her parents after everything she'd been through. The thought, however, that this could be the end was confronting. She still wasn't ready to see her father, not only for her sake but for his. There was no way of knowing how she'd react being faced with him again, or whatever old feelings it would bring to the fore. She didn't feel capable of pretending nothing had happened, but neither did she want to vent her anger towards him when he wasn't strong enough to hear it.

If this was the end, she'd lost the chance not only to build bridges, but to even say goodbye.

Angelo must have seen the panic in her eyes

as he rubbed her arm reassuringly. 'He hasn't got any worse. Your mother just gets a bit upset after seeing him.'

Inés was grateful for the reassurance bringing her heart rate back to an acceptable level. 'Of course. I'm glad she has someone to turn to. I'm just not ready to be that shoulder she needs right now, so thank you, Ángelo.'

'Without sounding as though I'm getting involved in your personal business again, do you think you'll visit your father before it's too late?' It wasn't the accusatory tone he'd used with her previously on the subject of her relationship with her parents. Ángelo was talking to her with the same tenderness he'd showed her mother and she appreciated his concern.

Inés shrugged. 'At some point. When I'm ready to face him, I suppose. In time I could come to forgive him, but I'll never forget.'

'But there might not be that much time left,' Ángelo reminded her.

Nevertheless, Inés wasn't going to be rushed into a decision. This time she wanted to dictate what happened next in her life without another man's interference.

'I know, but that's between me and my conscience. Now, is there anything else I can do for you?' Inés switched her computer on to let him know she was ready to start work and that this conversation was done.

While she appreciated everything he'd done for her parents and that family meant a lot to him, she wasn't going to justify her actions any more. She'd shared a lot of very personal information with him that she hadn't told anyone before, yet she knew nothing about him before he'd come to the family practice. He might be a friend and confidant to her mother, but he was just a work colleague to her.

'No. That's all right. I suppose we should get ready for the day ahead.' Ángelo turned on his heels and the sound of his office door closing soon followed.

Inés smiled to herself, feeling as though she'd got the upper hand for once. From now on she was going to do things on her own terms and Ángelo was just going to have to get used to it.

'I'll see you again next week to make sure the medication agrees with you, Mr Morris.' Ángelo saw his patient to the door. An English tourist who'd decided to stay on holiday indefinitely, only to find he was allergic to mosquito bites.

It had been a busy day with little time in between appointments to chat. The only conversation he'd really had with Inés was when she informed him that their cardiac patient was recovering well in hospital thanks to their intervention. It was probably for the best that his interaction with Inés was kept to a minimum for now in case he said anything else to irritate her.

He was doing his best not to antagonise her by interfering, but he so wanted her to find peace with her family before she might come to regret it. By coming all this way, helping out at the clinic, he could tell that their relationship wasn't completely beyond repair. For her sake, as well as her mother and father's, he hoped they could build some bridges. At least she still had a family. What was left of his had gone their own ways and, try as he might, he couldn't get his brothers to be a part of his life. He missed them. He missed being part of a family and he wouldn't wish that on Inés, or anyone else.

Suddenly the quiet of his office was interrupted by the sound of shouting and screaming outside, followed by Marie bursting in through the door.

'You need to come quick. There's been a fire in the building down the street. You and Inés are needed.' She'd apparently relayed the message to Inés, too, who had grabbed her medical bag and met him in the hall.

At least he knew from here they would set aside their differences and come together for whatever had unfolded outside.

The area they were in looked like a residential area, but it was a mixture of private businesses, like dentists and solicitors. However, at the end of the street there was a small family-run grocery shop packed to the rafters with all manner of foods and essentials. To Ángelo's horror, it was this small detached building which had smoke billowing out of the door and windows.

'It's the Garcias' place,' he told Inés, unsure if she had ventured into the shop yet, though it was an everyday stop for most people in the area. Him included. It was easier to grab something to eat from the local store on the way home from work rather than venturing to the big supermarkets, even if it cost a little more. He'd come to know the couple who ran the business, along with their children and knew how hard they worked to make a living. This would surely devastate them.

'You know them?' Inés hurried down the street alongside him as the other residents and business owners emerged, likely as worried for their own properties as the one on fire.

'Everyone here does. Your mother said they've been here for years.' Though obviously they must have moved in some time after Inés had moved to England since she didn't appear to know them.

Thankfully when they reached the bottom of

the street, Mr and Mrs Garcia were already outside, covered in soot and coughing.

'Has someone phoned the fire brigade and the paramedics?' Ángelo asked a gathering crowd.

Once he'd been assured the emergency services were on their way, he and Inés were able to focus on the injuries the middle-aged couple had sustained.

'I'm Inés. I'm a doctor. Can you tell me where it hurts?' Inés got down on to the ground beside Mrs Garcia to check her over and Ángelo focused on Mr Garcia who was coughing heavily.

'My hands. I tried to put the fire out myself.' Mrs Garcia held up her hands which were red raw and Inés immediately started to dress the burns. She carefully cleaned the wounds and applied a sterile dressing with gauze and tape to hold it in place.

Ángelo focused his attention on the male patient, seeing that Inés had everything in hand next to him.

'Can't. Breathe.' Mr Garcia's reddened eyes were wide with fear as he fought for breath.

'It's the smoke in your lungs. Don't panic. The paramedics will be here soon and we'll get you some oxygen.' Ángelo tried to calm him down so he could make a proper assessment.

The smoke he'd inhaled would irritate his lungs, causing swelling, and could block oxygen from entering the bloodstream. However, panicking was going to make his symptoms worse, as understandable as it was after being through such a traumatic event.

Ángelo tested his pulse, which was beating frantically under his touch. Beneath the soot and smoke, Mr Garcia's skin was pale and clammy. A cold sweat breaking out all over.

'Inés, I think he's going into shock…' Ángelo was able to grab the patient before he fell back on to the ground and injured himself further.

Inés came to assist Ángelo to gently lower Mr Garcia's head on to the ground.

'Mr Garcia, we need you to keep your eyes open for us until the ambulance gets here. Look, your wife is beside you.' She did her best to keep him responsive, talking to him continuously.

Ángelo pulled over an upturned bin and lifted the patient's legs on to it, improving the blood supply to his vital organs.

Inés loosened Mr Garcia's clothing to ensure it wasn't constricting blood flow. 'He's cold, Ángelo.'

If shock wasn't treated immediately and effectively, it could lead to permanent organ damage, or even death. Not something he wanted to happen to anyone he knew, nor in front of other residents.

'Has anyone got a blanket, or a coat? Anything?' he shouted to the rubberneckers around them. With no response, Ángelo pulled off his shirt and draped it over the patient. The best he could do for now and hopefully enough to keep him warm until help arrived.

'Very innovative.' Inés glanced at him, making him very aware that he was now topless. He saw the half-smile tugging at her mouth and wished he'd thought to wear an undershirt this morning.

Thankfully the blare of the ambulance sirens sounded nearby, taking the focus off his partial nudity.

'Just hold in there for us, Mr Garcia,' he told the man, whose breathing was becoming more and more laboured.

At least the paramedics would be able to get him on oxygen and administer pain relief on the way to the hospital.

'You'll have to go with your husband to the hospital, Mrs Garcia, to have those burns assessed. Try to keep him awake. Just talk to him,' Inés coached her patient. Even though she'd dressed the wounds, there was always a chance of complications and the couple needed hospital treatment.

Ángelo met with the attending paramedics to relay events and the treatment they'd administered so far. Then he stood back and let them take over. Inés came to stand next to him as they watched the couple being transferred into the back of the ambulance. By now the fire brigade had arrived and were moving people out of the area so they could tackle the blaze. The air was thick with smoke, making his eyes and throat burn. When he turned to look at Inés he could see that her eyes were red and streaming, too.

'Let's get back to the clinic and get cleaned up. We've done our bit.' He reached out to take her hand. A subconscious gesture to show solidarity for what they'd just been through together. He hadn't expected her to take it and follow him back into the clinic.

As odd as it may have appeared as they walked hand in hand up the street, Ángelo still topless, and both smudged with dirt and soot, it felt natural. Comfortable. A few days ago he would never have imagined even being civil to one another. Now, Inés was a part of his working day, as well as his relationship with her parents. He'd spent so long building his career, focused on financial stability, that he'd forgotten how nice it was to let someone else help pick up the slack. To give his hand a reassuring squeeze and remind him he wasn't on his own.

He was beginning to wonder why he was still waiting to find that special someone when he had the rest of his life in order.

* * *

Inés was emotionally drained, yet her body was thrumming with the energy burst which always accompanied any medical drama. It would be some time before she came down from the adrenalin high. Not helped by the fact Ángelo had her hand clasped tightly in his.

She hadn't resisted when he'd reached out to her, keen to have that comfort from the only person who knew how she felt in moments like this. How every interaction, no matter the outcome, reserved a place in her heart as well as her head. Something Marty never seemed to understand when the only thing that mattered to him was how good he looked at his job. More interested in praise and plaudits than saving lives. Although she'd only been here for a matter of days, she could tell Ángelo was more invested in his patients than his ego. A refreshing change in her orbit.

Both she and Ángelo went into the treatment room to clean up, standing side by side at the sink, splashing water over their faces.

'Sorry,' she said, as she splashed some water on to his chest. Then she was forced to apologise once she realised she was trying to wipe it off with her hand. Essentially pawing at his chest like a member of a hen party at a male strip show.

'It's okay.' He seemed amused by seeing her flustered. A condition she was having trouble controlling when he was so close and half-naked.

All of that exercise seemed to be doing wonders for his physique when he was so taut beneath her fingertips. It didn't hurt that he had that little smattering of dark hair outlining his pectoral muscles either.

He washed his hands and Inés watched, mesmerised at every flex of the muscles in his strong arms. There was just something about him that made her want those arms wrapped around her, protecting her. Though she knew it would be a long time before she got close to any man again, Ángelo was beginning to make her believe that not all of them were out to hurt her. So far she'd seen nothing but good intentions from Ángelo, even if she'd been resentful of his presence here at first.

Before she could get too carried away singing his praises, that scared inner voice of the woman who'd been hurt too many times reminded her that she couldn't trust her judgement where men were concerned. She'd thought that Marty was kind and generous and she'd fallen for his good looks, too. This wasn't the time for making more of the same mistakes and she would have to keep reminding herself why she was here. It certainly wasn't to be blinded by another handsome man.

'Look at the state of you two. I found some old clothes of mine and Juan's in the cupboard you can change into.' Inés's mother bustled into the room and handed over the folded clothes she'd been carrying.

'Thanks, Mama.' Inés took them gratefully, doing her best not to baulk at the garish patterns.

'How are the Garcias? I hope they're going to be okay,' Mrs de la Fuente fretted.

'They've inhaled a lot of smoke and suffered burns, but with hospital treatment they should make a full recovery.' Ángelo did his best to put her mother's mind at rest even though things hadn't been straightforward.

'I'm sure they have you to thank for that,' her mother effused.

'I'm just glad Inés was there, too. She's been invaluable these past few days.' Ángelo's words, along with her mother's smile, gave Inés a warm glow inside.

It had been a long time since she'd felt appreciated and it was an unfamiliar, yet welcome, feeling. One of Marty's tricks to keep her under his control had been to undermine her at any given opportunity. Whittling away at her self-confidence so she felt even more reliant on him. It had taken her to leave the country before she'd realised just how he'd been able to manipulate her. Ángelo didn't appear to be threatened by her at all in a professional capacity. Seeming content to share the spotlight with her, with no need to put her down for the sake of his own ego. Comfortable enough in his own skin that he didn't see the need to exert any control or influence over her.

Perhaps that's what she found attractive about him. Not the lean body, deep brown eyes, or dark wavy hair.

'Well, I'll let you two get changed and I'll get the place closed up.' Her mother made a swift exit, leaving them standing awkwardly together.

'I'm not sure it's your style.' Inés held up the nineties-style paisley patterned shirt which was a far cry from Ángelo's usual conservative wardrobe.

He held it up and inspected it with a tilt of his head. 'I don't know. A life-or-death situation can give you a different perspective on the world. Perhaps it's time I lived a little dangerously.'

Inés watched as he shrugged it on, envious of the silky fabric caressing his muscular torso.

'Your turn,' he said, nodding at the chiffon pink shirt she was holding.

Ángelo was teasing her, daring her, and Inés wanted to show she was up to any challenge these days. There was no more being afraid to do what she wanted. Right now she wanted him to watch her the way she'd been watching him.

To see that spark of desire she'd felt when he'd taken her hand and stripped off his shirt.

Maintaining eye contact, she undid her blouse. Button by button. Inch by inch. Saw his eyes darken and his smile falter. For once she felt as though she had power and it was a potent aphrodisiac.

She let her top fall to the floor, revealing her lacy white bra to his gaze. Then she pulled the chiffon monstrosity over her head and let it fall over her body.

Ángelo took a step forward and she held her breath, waiting for him to touch her. He reached out and took hold of the ribbon hanging loosely at her throat and tied it into a bow.

'Beautiful,' he said, his voice unusually gravelly.

'If you're a fan of hideous eighties fashion...'

'I wasn't talking about the blouse...'

Inés's pulse leapt, a silent squeal emanating inside her as he looked at her with such a hunger. It felt good to be wanted, to be seen as a prize, instead of something to be subjugated.

'You two look good. Go on, I'll lock up. It's been a long day for both of you.' Inés's mother arrived before anything other than lingering looks had time to manifest.

Probably for the best. Inés didn't know how long she'd be here for, but she needed her job.

A foolish fling with a co-worker wasn't going to help set her life back on the right track. All it would do would be to cause her more complications she didn't need.

'I need a drink.' Ángelo backed away with a sigh of what Inés hoped was regret as her mother put a stop to whatever had been happening between them, and disappeared again.

'Me, too.' Anything to drown out the hormones which were making themselves very vocal about how fit they thought Ángelo suddenly was.

'There's a bar down the end of the street if you want to call in? It's always hard to wind down after something like that happens. The fire, I mean.' Ángelo didn't seem his usual cool, calm, collected self. Although he wasn't exactly asking her out on a date, even the suggestion was clearly out of his comfort zone.

Hers, too.

Marty had never permitted her to socialise with her work colleagues when they'd met up outside work for drinks, or birthday dinners. It seemed ridiculous now that she'd capitulated to that, but she hadn't wanted to upset him and it had been easier to turn down all invitations rather than have a row after the event. In the end, people had stopped asking her to join them so it no longer represented a problem.

86 SPANISH DOC TO HEAL HER

'Why not?' Simply doing something spontaneous like going for a drink with a colleague felt empowering. It also gave her a boost thinking that Marty would've hated it.

She tried not to read too much into the fact Ángelo had even asked her out.

CHAPTER FIVE

'ARE YOU SURE you want to go in here?' Ángelo eyed the small bar warily. It wasn't one he frequented. Run by a British expat, it was usually full of drunken tourists watching the football. He preferred quiet, authentic Spanish establishments which served tapas with their drinks instead of greasy fry ups.

Inés gave him the side eye. 'I've spent ten years living in England. I'm used to this. I like the atmosphere in a good old British pub. Let's face it, that's what it is. They've just relocated it to the sun.'

He screwed up his face. It wasn't his favourite place in the world. The locals didn't always get along with the expat community since not many of them made an effort to integrate into their new surroundings. Some had been here twenty years or more and never even learned the language, relying on the fact that most Spanish spoke some English.

Though he supposed he shouldn't be too critical when that was part of the reason their practice was so successful.

Inés looked so excited by the idea he didn't want to disappoint her either. She hadn't had an easy time since arriving and he supposed one night out wasn't going to kill him.

He sighed, resigning himself to an evening with drunken tourists. 'If this is what you want…'

'It is.' Inés batted her long, dark eyelashes at him and he was putty in her hands.

Ángelo increasingly found himself wanting to please her, to put that gorgeous smile on her face which had been in scarce supply since her arrival.

The pub clientele had already spilled out on to the outside balcony, all deep in high-spirited conversation, clutching their drinks. They had to push through the crowd to reach the bar.

'What can I get you?' the smiley blonde lady behind the bar greeted them.

'A beer, please,' Inés shouted over his shoulder.

'Make that two,' he added.

'No problem. Take a seat and I'll bring them over.' The barmaid directed them to a little table in the corner of the bar which wasn't currently occupied and they sat down before anyone else spotted it.

'Are you really uncomfortable in here?' Inés asked as they had time to take in the decor which was covered in Union Jack flags and English football shirts. 'It just reminds me of when I first moved to England and that sense of freedom I felt. I partied a bit too much in the beginning, before studies, among other things, took all my focus. It's been a while since I've been able to let my hair down the way I want, but we can go somewhere else if you'd rather?'

It was sweet of her to be concerned for him, but he wasn't bothered in the slightest. Glad to be sitting here chilling out with Inés.

'It's fine, but next time I'm taking you somewhere you can get back in touch with your roots,' he teased. Then he realised he'd promised another night out together. Thankfully she didn't look horrified by the suggestion, even though he hadn't been aware he was already thinking that far ahead.

'Hey, I'm half-English, you know.' Inés nudged him playfully.

'I know, but when was the last time you listened to some Spanish guitar, or danced a flamenco?'

She looked thoughtful. 'I can't remember. You might have a point...'

'That's quite a list of things we need to reacquaint you with that we're building. I hope you're sticking around long enough to do everything.' It was wishful thinking on his part. Especially when he appeared to be making plans for them to hang out together in the future.

He found himself wanting to give her reasons to stay, not looking forward to the day when she decided to move on. Not only had she proven herself as an excellent doctor, but he liked being in her company. Unlike when he'd been with his ex, Camila, he didn't feel as though he had to prove himself in any way. Though, he reminded himself, Inés was not a potential future partner. As long as he remembered that she was worth her weight in gold at the practice and any romantic inclinations he might have could send her running, he should hopefully manage to avoid temptation.

'Two beers.' Thankfully their drinks arrived before he, or Inés, was forced to make any commitment.

He handed over payment, but the blonde stared at the two of them. 'Are you on your way to an eighties party or something?'

'It was bad taste day at work,' Inés joked, sending the barmaid away with a bemused expression.

Ángelo loved the way she wasn't self-conscious about going out like this. Not everyone would be happy about being seen in public with their make-up washed off, wearing their mother's old clothes. It showed she was comfortable not only in herself, but around him. Things between them had definitely mellowed since their first meeting.

'So where do you usually go, if you don't come here after work?' Inés asked, taking a sip from her beer.

'I'm not one for going out much.'

'Not at all?'

He shook his head. 'Not really. Not since I started working here. I've been so focused on work I haven't really left time for socialising.'

'You don't have a significant other?'

'Not at the minute. Not for some time, actually.'

'Bad break up?' She looked at him sympathetically.

He thought back to the last woman he'd been seeing and couldn't even remember her name—it had been such a long time ago and nothing more than a casual arrangement. Camila's rejection had made him wary of giving his heart to anyone again. He'd been willing to devote himself to her for ever, but she'd found him wanting. Not rich, or successful enough, for her to consider being with long term. Since then he made sure not to tie himself down, or make promises of a happy ever after to anyone. Including himself. At least, not until he had all of the building blocks in place for the foundation of his perfect, happy family.

'Not particularly. Relationships just haven't been my focus.'

'You're not interested in marriage and children?'

'On the contrary. Which is why I didn't want anything serious until I had a steady job and financial security. I won't settle down unless I know I can provide for my family. Both financially and emotionally.' Perhaps now that he had both he might actually open up his life and share it with someone.

He'd been so caught up in work he'd put his love life on the back burner and he wondered if his growing attraction to Inés was simply a symptom of that. She was the only woman in his life at present and he needed to expand his horizons beyond the clinic. By her own admission she wasn't making any promises about sticking around and if he was going to go all in with someone he wanted to be sure they weren't going to leave him the way everyone else in his life had.

'Very sensible.' There was a twinkle in her eye as she took another swig from her bottle and he was sure she was teasing him.

'Well, I know what it's like to grow up in an

unstable environment.' He washed down the hint of bitterness which had begun to swell inside him. It wasn't that he blamed anyone for the circumstances he'd grown up in, but he didn't wish it for his own family.

'I'm sorry. You never talk much about your family.'

Ángelo shrugged. He hadn't meant to either, but with a drop of alcohol, and his defences down, it was easy to open up to Inés. Particularly because she'd already shared a little of her family circumstances with him, so he didn't feel so vulnerable opening up a little bit to a listening ear.

'My mother left when I was very young. Father did his best to raise me and my brothers, but he had his own demons with alcohol.' He tipped his bottle with a sardonic grin. Thankfully he'd never had any real vices. Likely because he'd seen the damage it could do to a person and those around them.

'I'm sorry. I guess I imagined you had the perfect family because you were so keen for me to reconcile with mine.'

Ángelo flinched at the reminder he'd butted in where he had no business interfering, when he didn't have all the facts. And because he hadn't known Inés at all at the time he'd tried to tell her how she should be behaving towards her parents.

He knew from experience not everyone reacted the same way as he did to certain situations, especially where family was involved.

'I can't apologise enough for that. It was something ingrained in me from my *abuela*. My father wasn't really capable of raising three sons on his own, so she picked up a lot of the slack. According to her, family was everything. No matter what happened. She despised my mother for leaving, but she had to put up with a lot. My father could get very violent when he'd had too much to drink. Which was often.'

'I'm so sorry, Ángelo. I had no idea.' Inés reached out and took his hand, giving him a sympathetic squeeze.

Normally he would have shrugged off any outward display of pity, not believing he'd suffered any more than most growing up in difficult circumstances. Yet, he was glad of her touch. Her comfort. The connection they were making. He let her hold on to him as long as she wanted.

'It's not something I usually share with people.' In truth, he had no idea why he was even telling her now, other than the knowledge that it would give her a greater understanding of the person he was, perhaps.

'Well, thank you for trusting me.' She held eye contact and gave his hand an extra squeeze, but didn't let go. 'Did he…was he violent with you?'

It was a probing, personal question that set his teeth on edge and made his jaw tighten. He didn't want to besmirch his family name, this was his father they were talking about. But he also knew Inés wasn't merely wanting gossip. She cared. For the first time in his life he found himself wanting to tell that story. Acknowledging that it had happened and he'd got through it. It hadn't been easy, but it had made him the man he was today.

He simply nodded, not going into detail. It was enough for Inés to gasp, her hand leaving his to cover her mouth. Inexplicably, he felt tears burning the back of his eyes. It was alien and disturbing. He wasn't someone who tended to feel sorry for himself, or dwell on the past. It was all about the future for him and the family he hoped to have some day.

Perhaps it was this feeling of vulnerability which was making him emotional. Seeing himself through Inés's eyes as the young boy being beaten by his drunken father. It could even be the fact that for the first time someone was really seeing him beyond the successful doctor he'd become. Getting to know the real Ángelo that he kept hidden from most people. Even her parents didn't know about his past.

He waited for the look of horror, the sympathetic noises and being told what a brave boy he'd been. Instead, Inés shocked him completely, turning and pulling him into a bear hug. He didn't remember ever being squeezed so hard, as though she was trying to make him feel all the love and compassion he'd never had growing up from his parents.

He revelled in it. In the comfort she provided, and the feel of her in his arms. With his head buried in her hair, he could smell the smoke from the fire mixed in with her strawberry-scented shampoo. A reminder of their day and everything they'd been through together so far in such a short space of time. When his body began to react to her soft curves against him, however, he was forced to pull away. Embarrassed that he was responding inappropriately to her gesture.

Inés didn't let the awkward silence persist for too long. Though he might have preferred it to the alternative.

'What about your mother?'

Ángelo shook his head. 'I contacted her after my father died, but she didn't want to be reminded of the life she'd had with us. She moved shortly after that and didn't pass on a forwarding address so I lost touch again. I heard later she'd died.'

'And your brothers? Are you still in contact with them?'

Ángelo hadn't meant to go down this particular rabbit hole with her, but it was too late now. Inés seemed genuinely interested, caring about him and the relationships he'd lost, too. If he refused to answer her questions, it would only make things difficult between them again when he was just getting used to having her around.

'No. I've tried, but they have their own lives and don't feel as though they have any ties here any more. As soon as they were old enough they left home and never looked back.' It had been difficult for him in so many ways. At times he envied them their freedom, but it also felt like a punishment that his family had gradually been taken away from him.

'You stayed with your father?'

He knew it probably sounded ridiculous given the circumstances, but he still didn't regret it. 'I cared for him right until the end. My brothers couldn't understand why I stayed. Sometimes I don't either, but he was my only family left. I was all he had and I wasn't going to simply walk away.'

'It's not easy to make that call and sever that connection when you've been conditioned to play a certain role for so long.' As she took a swig of beer, he got the impression they weren't just talking about him any more.

He supposed that sense of duty to family at

all costs his *abuela* had instilled in him meant he'd put up with a lot of bad behaviour he didn't need to. If he'd done what Inés and his brothers had done and walked away, prioritised himself instead of someone who'd never cared for him, he could have had a different life. He might still have his brothers in his life. Maybe even a wife and children of his own. Perhaps that was the family he should have been concentrating on instead of the toxic one he'd clung on to for too long.

'But you did. You broke away and started a new life. That's incredibly brave.' They clearly had different backgrounds and attitudes, but he understood what it took to make those big decisions. After all, she'd moved away from everything she'd ever known to a different country. She hadn't taken the easy way out either.

Inés's expression turned into something inscrutable. Dark. As though he'd said something really offensive. She even opened her mouth as if to say something, but took another sip of beer instead. He hadn't meant to upset her, he'd been complimenting her, not intending to patronise. But before he could apologise for whatever faux pas he'd made, the barmaid came over and set a sheet of paper and a pen on their table.

'You've picked a good night. The karaoke's

starting in a minute. Write down your request and the microphone is all yours.'

Just when Ángelo thought things couldn't get any worse…

Inés was grateful for the distraction. She couldn't bear Ángelo praising her bravery, knowing that she'd walked straight into another controlling relationship. Without the interruption she might have told him about Marty and what that new life became over the last ten years. She didn't want to let him keep believing she was some strong, courageous warrior woman, when she'd been anything but that. Neither did she want him to look at her differently once he realised she was actually weak and pathetic enough to hand control of her life to another man.

She supposed she had eventually found the courage to walk away from him, too, and now she just wanted to put it all behind her. A night out would hopefully help her do that.

She was grateful he'd been able to open up to her about his past, no matter how painful that must have been for him. It was no wonder he couldn't reconcile himself with her estrangement from her family, when he'd tried to so hard to keep his together. Though it sounded psychologically damaging to him having stayed at home. It seemed their parents' behaviour had deeply affected them both. They could both do with a night out, cutting loose.

'I'll get us another drink.' She scribbled their names down on the sheet and handed it back before Ángelo realised what she was up to.

'Two tequila shots, please.' Inés had to shout to be heard as the karaoke started and the place was filled with the sound of tuneless screeching from a middle-aged woman who'd clearly had one too many glasses of sangria.

'Tequila?' Ángelo's eyebrows shot up as she brought the drinks back to the table.

A group of young women got up next and gave a clearly well-rehearsed routine which got the whole crowd singing along.

'I think you're going to need it.' Inés clinked her glass to his and threw her head back to swallow the fiery liquid.

'Next up we have Inés and Ángelo,' the MC announced and everyone in the bar began clapping.

Everyone except Ángelo, who was looking at her with abject horror. 'You didn't.'

'I did,' she said with a grin.

Although she wasn't an introvert, on the rare occasions she had been out with her colleagues, before Marty put a stop to it, she'd enjoyed karaoke nights. It had given her a sense of liberation just to get up and make a fool of herself without the fear of recriminations. Marty would've been horrified if he'd witnessed her strutting herself on stage after a couple of wines. This didn't have the same space to move as the bars they'd frequented in London, but it meant a smaller audience to their attempt to sing.

She reckoned Ángelo needed to sample a little of that freedom and break out of his comfort zone for a while. He didn't seem to have a life beyond work and she knew how that felt. Even if he appeared to have isolated himself, rather than because he had a controlling partner. The scars from their pasts had a lot to answer for when they were still letting what had happened prevent them from moving forward.

The barmaid produced two microphones. Inés grabbed one, but Ángelo knocked his drink back before he accepted the other one.

'I can't believe you've betrayed me like this, Inés.' He was frowning at her, but he was taking part regardless and that made her happy.

She had chosen a cheesy eighties duet for them to sing and Ángelo was staring at the screen intently, waiting for the words to appear. It was a song she knew by heart. Mostly because of the repetitive lyrics reminiscent of the era.

Inés blew him a kiss and launched into the opening line. She was convinced she might have to sing his part to when he kept giving her the side eye and shaking his head. For all she knew he might not be familiar with the song. Then he suddenly launched into his verse and surprised her with his fabulous rendition. Inés smiled at him as they harmonised the chorus together and by the time the instrumental bridge came, they'd settled into the song. Ángelo even twirled her around the floor.

Back in his arms, having him sing words of love and being together for ever, it was easy to believe they were a couple. Even for Inés. But all too soon the song came to an end and they broke apart to the sound of applause.

Inés was buzzing from the thrill of the whole thing by the time they sat down. Ángelo grabbed another two beers before he joined her and she waited for a scolding.

'Well, that was unexpected,' he simply said with a laugh.

It wasn't until he smiled at her that she realised she'd been waiting for a negative reaction. That tension back in her body that she used to experience when she'd done something to annoy Marty. He would've been furious if she'd ever dared to pull such a stunt on him, but Ángelo took it in good humour. Letting her relax and enjoy the rest of her drink without worrying about the consequences of her actions.

Clearly taking control of everything wasn't as

important to him as it had been to every other man in her life.

'Admit it, you had fun.' She knew she had.

'It wasn't as awful as I imagined,' he conceded.

'And you can sing.' It had been a revelation, along with the fact that he was capable of loosening up.

'Usually just in the shower.'

Now he'd planted the image of him naked under water, Inés couldn't seem to shake it out of her head. The more time she spent with him, the more he seemed to linger in her thoughts. Now she'd seen him half-naked it was even easier to have inappropriate thoughts about him, even if nothing could come of it. She wasn't in the market for a relationship when she was simply trying to get back on her feet. It would be a while before she would ever trust a man not to try to take over her life again.

Ángelo had already made it clear that he was hoping for a relationship and a family in his future, but she wasn't ready to think that far ahead. So she certainly wasn't looking to start something with her colleague who had as much family baggage as she had.

'I hope I'm getting a percentage of your future earnings for discovering your talent.' Inés tried to cleanse her dirty mind by bringing some levity to the occasion.

Except Ángelo's hearty chuckle only added to his appeal. The warm sound reaching deep inside her to tug at parts of her she'd deemed out of bounds.

'I wouldn't give up your day job. I'm certainly not. I think I'll retire at the top, thanks.' He raised his bottle in toast. Inés clinked hers to it.

'This isn't a regular occurrence for you, then?'

Ángelo nearly spat out his drink. 'No. It's been a while since I did any socialising. Not since I joined your father's practice anyway. It hasn't been a priority for me.'

Inés knew the feeling. It was nice, though, just to be able to have a drink with a colleague without fear of reprisals. Perhaps they could do a bit more of it. She might even make some new friends along the way so Ángelo wasn't her sole go-to for company. If she'd learned anything, it was not to rely too heavily on one person. Then they couldn't take advantage of her.

'It's been a while for me, too. Socialising, I mean.' She felt her cheeks flush at the thought he could've misinterpreted her comment for something more personal. Though it had been a while since she'd shared her bed either.

Given Ángelo's apparent focus on his career, she got the impression his love life hadn't been a priority for him. Perhaps that was part of the attraction, knowing that he didn't represent a threat. Ángelo was safe, because he wasn't interested in her, or a relationship.

Yet she was sure every now and then he looked at her with something more than a simple curiosity. Especially when they'd been dancing together and singing about loving each other for ever. The romantic in her wondered what that would be like, but the realist reminded her she'd fallen victim to those fantasies before. Only to find herself trapped with no say in her own life.

It was probably better to keep her thoughts, and her relationship with Ángelo, strictly at work.

'I should probably go home. It's getting late.' She drained her beer in a hurry, even though she would have preferred to take her time over it. It had been too long since she'd enjoyed a night out like this and it was ironic that she wanted to leave because she was in danger of having too much fun. She didn't want it to become a habit. At least not with Ángelo.

'I'll walk you home.' He finished his beer and stood up.

'No. You don't have to. It's not that far.' This wasn't the plan. She was supposed to be putting some distance between them, not finding a way for them to be alone together.

He frowned at her. 'There is no way I'm leaving you to walk back alone, in the dark. Your parents would never forgive me.'

Although he was half joking, Inés knew he was right. Neither of them would ever hear the end of it if her mother found out she'd walked back on her own. Not in a controlling way, but in an 'I'm an over-protective Mama' way. It didn't matter that she was almost thirty years old, or that she'd spent ten years living in London. Here, she was still her mother's baby and she'd been entrusted to Ángelo's care. Neither she, nor Ángelo, were going to take on her wrath for the sake of a five-minute walk.

Resigned, she followed him, only pausing to wave a farewell to the blonde behind the bar.

'*Gracias,*' she called across the room before another singer had a chance to take the mic.

'Hope we see you next week!'

Inés resisted the urge to tell her this was a one-off. Probably because deep down she was hoping there would be a second non-date. Despite her vow to herself that she wouldn't get too attached to life here in Spain, still trying to maintain some emotional distance from her parents, it did have its attractions. As dangerous as her ponderings were, she wondered what it might be like if she stayed. Being around Ángelo, and the connection they'd made, had her starting to believe that not everyone was like Marty. That some day she might be ready to share her life with someone else. She just had to be one hundred per cent sure that the next time she opened her heart up to anyone else, that they wouldn't take advantage of her.

They'd just made it to the bottom of the steps, dodging around the inebriated clientele congregated around the entrance, when they heard a high-pitched squeal behind them. Inés turned around to see a dishevelled woman in her twenties lying in a heap on the pavement at the bottom of the steps.

'Oww!' The injured party was rubbing at her ankle, one of her sparkly high heels lying broken nearby.

'Ángelo?' Inés touched him lightly on the arm to alert him to the situation, doing her best to ignore the warmth of his skin beneath her fingertips. Every time they made physical contact she felt as though an electric charge was running through her body. Not the ideal scenario when she worked so closely with him. She was in danger of short-circuiting one of these days. Especially when he already seemed to be playing havoc with her hormones.

'Are you okay?' They both turned back to offer their assistance, with Ángelo addressing

108   SPANISH DOC TO HEAL HER

the casualty since Inés's thoughts had been pre-occupied elsewhere.

'My heel snapped and I slid down the last few steps. I think I've twisted my ankle.' The young English woman didn't look too distressed though she was wincing. Judging by the smell of alcohol wafting from her, Inés suspected the pain was somewhat dulled by the cocktails they'd witnessed her party drinking inside the bar.

'What have you done, you daft mare?' One of her friends staggered out with her drink in hand, less than sympathetic to her plight.

'I'm having a lie down…what does it look like?'

Before the pair exchanged any more words, Inés and Ángelo moved to her side and tried to help her up.

'Can you walk on that foot?' Inés asked, encouraging her to try to put some weight on it to assess the damage.

A yelp of pain as the woman limped into Ángelo's arms soon told a story. Though her injury seemed quickly forgotten as she got up close and personal with Ángelo. '*Hola*, Handsome.'

He gave an embarrassed smile and Inés was surprised by the surge of jealousy she felt at another woman showing an interest in him. It was only natural, he was a good-looking man after all. But they'd grown so close, so quickly, she was already hating the thought of him being with anyone else. If she was going to be sticking around for any length of time, she was definitely going to have to get over that idea she had any claim on him. Inés certainly wouldn't appreciate it if Ángelo became possessive over her. At least, that's what she tried to convince herself.

'We should get you back inside.' Inés took charge, lifting one of the woman's arms from around Ángelo's shoulders on to her own.

Between them they provided support on either side of the woman and took the steps slowly so they didn't all end up in a heap.

'Patient incoming!' the very helpful friend yelled, clearing a path through the bar so they could deposit their new friend on to a seat.

'Have you got a first-aid kit?' Ángelo asked the blonde barmaid who was clearly surprised to see them back so soon.

'I'm not sure what we have in it,' she said as she placed the small, green box on to the table.

'Thanks.' Ángelo flashed that megawatt smile that brought him yet another blushing admirer.

'I think you've cut yourself.' Inés directed everyone's attention back to the young woman's injuries which she could see now included her arms and legs. The skin grazed and broken where she'd scraped against the steps.

'Ach, it's just a scratch.' Their patient shrugged

off Inés's concern, focusing on Ángelo who was feeling around her ankle.

'Can you rotate your ankle for me?' he asked, as Inés set about cleaning the abrasions with some antiseptic wipes.

The woman sucked in a sharp breath, then affected a babyish tone. 'It hurts.'

'But you can move it so I don't think anything is broken. It's likely just a sprain. I'll strap it up for now, but if there is any bruising or swelling I'd suggest you get it checked out at the hospital.' Ángelo took a bandage out of the first-aid kit and began to wind it around the foot.

'I'd advise wearing flat shoes for the rest of your trip, too.' Inés finished cleaning away the blood and grime from the superficial cuts and grazes, glad there were no serious injuries.

'Yeah. Alcohol and high heels don't mix well.' Ángelo gave her a knowing smile and her heart did a somersault.

It was nice to have the back up and Inés realised she'd been so busy trying to keep herself protected that she was missing out on the best part of being in a medical practice. Working alongside fellow medical professionals had been the best part of her life for a long time. The one place she'd felt able to be herself, even if Marty had curtailed the idea of her socialising beyond the work environment. Ángelo was content to facilitate both where Inés was concerned. Happy to co-operate on medical matters and go out for a drink, without ever telling her what to do.

It was nice not having to be on edge all of the time. Simply free to exist.

Ángelo was everything she needed right now.

CHAPTER SIX

THEY PATCHED UP the young woman as best they could, but she seemed determined to carry on drinking regardless of her injuries. Ángelo and Inés left her with her bandaged foot propped on a stool and a microphone in her hand.

No matter how good he was at his job, Ángelo couldn't get rid of the feeling he'd got himself into a terrible mess where his personal life was concerned. Entirely because he'd had such a good time tonight in Inés's company. In a way he'd been glad when she'd decided to end it. Before they had too much to drink and he was tempted to throw caution to the wind and act on the attraction he felt towards her. One which had been steadily growing. Even more so now that he'd seen this carefree side of her which had encouraged him to shake loose for a while, too.

He'd almost forgotten how to have fun in his pursuit of stability in his life. Something he'd have to rediscover if he ever hoped to find himself a long-term partner. It was all well and good having a secure financial status, but he was going to have to have some kind of social life happening if he was ever going to meet someone.

Someone other than Inés.

As much as he liked her, getting involved wouldn't be a sensible idea. Apart from being a co-worker, and daughter of the people he was closest to, she wasn't in the right head space to be what he was looking for. What he needed.

Except there was no way his conscience, or her mother, would let her walk home alone.

'The lighting isn't the best here. Until you're used to the place there's a chance you could slip and break an ankle. Also, it's prime territory for muggers.' The uneven footway wasn't fit for pedestrians. Especially those who'd been drinking.

Inés shuddered. He hadn't meant to scare her, but warn her of the danger. The place had likely changed since she'd last been here and, if she was ever to come this way again on her own, he wanted her to be prepared.

'And you're going to protect me?'

'If I have to,' he said through gritted teeth, knowing if anyone dared lay a finger on her, he'd defend her. She had a way of making him feel protective towards her and he had to be careful not to overstep in case she saw him as just another dominating male. The truth was, he kind of felt responsible for her. She was the daughter of good friends, a colleague, and someone he'd apparently come to see as a confidant.

'I see you're also going to save me from any out-of-control vehicles, too.' She nodded towards his position beside her, on the outside, so anything coming would hit him first.

It hadn't been a conscious choice. Simply a natural instinct to safeguard her.

'If I have to.' He used the same jokey tone to hide his genuine concern for her safety. Ángelo had the feeling she wouldn't appreciate it.

'You're too good to me. Thanks, by the way, for getting up and singing with me. I know I put you on the spot.'

'You didn't leave me much choice.' He narrowed his eyes at her. 'It would have been excruciating to have to watch and listen to you doing a duet on your own.'

She gave him a playful slap on the arm. 'Hey, we can't all have perfect pitch. Though I do make up for it in enthusiasm.'

Inés launched into another hearty chorus of their party piece, uncaring about showing herself up in front of passing traffic. He loved that sense of freedom she had. It was infectious and soon he found himself joining in. The two of them walking along in the dark, singing like any other couple who'd had a fun night out together.

They even recreated their impromptu dance, where Ángelo spun her around before taking her in his arms for a waltz. Her smile was as broad as his, even though he knew he was in dangerous territory. Especially when the singing ended, but they hadn't moved out of their dance hold, staring at one another while they clung together.

It would have been easy to lean in and kiss her. He wanted to. She was looking at him as though she was waiting for it. But he knew once he did there'd be no going back. It wasn't something they could simply forget about when they worked together every day. It would always be more than just a kiss and he wasn't sure if either of them wanted that right now.

He reluctantly released her and kept on walking, trying not to pay any heed to the intensity of the moment which had just passed between them.

'They call this Cat Bridge, you know,' he said as they crossed over the strip of wasteland below them which at one time had housed the water system for the area but had since been abandoned to local wildlife.

'Oh? Why's that?' Inés moved along with the change between them. She probably realised they'd been venturing on to dangerous ground, too.

'A lot of stray and wild cats have taken it over.

The locals leave out food and water for them. Your mother included.' He knew it encouraged the felines around the property, but he was glad that they were being looked after in some form.

'I'm sure my father loves that.'

'He doesn't know.' It was dawning on Ángelo now just how dominating Juan could be. He'd always taken it for granted that since it was his practice, he made the rules. With the information he'd gleaned from Inés he could see now how her mother deferred to him about everything. Secretly feeding stray cats was likely her one small act of rebellion. She wasn't as different from her daughter as she thought. That feisty spirit there in both of the de la Fuente women.

He knew what it was like to be stuck. Regardless that he'd voluntarily stayed with his father. In a way he'd felt indebted to the man for sticking around after his mother had left. Even if he hadn't been the greatest father. Love was a powerful motivator. He supposed it was the same for Inés's mother. No matter what happened, she couldn't bring herself to leave the man she loved. Inés had been braver than both of them.

'This is me.' Inés stopped outside the gates of her parents' villa.

Ángelo had been too wrapped up in his own thoughts to realise they'd reached their destination all too soon.

'You can let your mother know I got you home safely.'

Inés turned and clicked a button on her key fob to open the electric gates. 'You could come in and tell her yourself.'

Ángelo checked his watch. He doubted Marie was still awake and he was worried that if he accepted the invitation to accompany Inés inside, his vow not to kiss her might be tested. 'It's late. I wouldn't want to disturb her.'

Inés nodded. 'Well, thanks for a good night. I can't remember the last time I had so much fun.'

The twinkle in her eyes under the moonlight and the wide smile said she was being genuine. He felt exactly the same. If this had been a first date it would've been perfect. With a second definitely on the cards. That's what was making it so hard to walk away now. It wasn't every day he met someone he had such a great connection with. What a shame that nothing could come of it.

'Nor me. Thanks, Inés.' He leaned forward to give her a peck on the cheek. A brief kiss goodnight. Polite and respectful. A simple gesture of his gratitude for her company.

At least, that was how it started.

The second his lips touched her skin he was electrified. Zapped to life, the touch of her awakening parts of him that had lain dormant for too long. He was sure Inés felt it, too, as he watched her eyes flutter shut and she tilted her chin up towards him. Her full lips inviting him to taste her. Inside him, a silent groan heralded the last of his restraint snapping.

The alcohol he'd consumed, combined with the good time they'd had together, was starting to make him think this was a good idea. That one little kiss wasn't the end of the world. Merely the natural conclusion of a pleasant night out together.

He moved his mouth the short distance to cover hers and when she opened up to meet him, he was lost. With his defences well and truly breached, he unleashed the desire he'd been holding back since their first clash in the clinic. The passion awakened inside him by her touch, her taste, only making him want more.

He pulled her close, deepening the kiss, her soft body crushed against the hardness of his. The little groans of delight coming from Inés, spurring him on in his pursuit. Mouths clashing, tongues teasing, they engaged in the kiss together with a passion he hadn't expected. It was only supposed to have been a goodnight peck, not foreplay. Yet this was exactly what it felt like. A promise of more to come and something he would've been very keen to explore.

When the electronic gates began to close, deciding that they'd taken too long, it was a wake-up call he probably needed.

'I should go.' He pulled away, trying to remember if there were security cameras. It would be a hard job explaining this to Marie and convincing her they weren't involved in some passionate love affair. Even if one mind-blowing kiss was trying to convince him it wouldn't be such a bad idea.

Inés took a wobbly step back, looking almost as dazed as he felt. 'Yeah. Um…goodnight. We should do this again some time. Or not.'

She backed into the still-closed gates and Ángelo had to suppress a smile, seeing that she'd been as knocked sideways by the kiss as he had.

'Probably not,' he said with more than a hint of sadness. As fun as it had been, he didn't want to risk his future at the practice by getting involved with Inés. Especially when she didn't know how long she was going to be sticking around for. He had a feeling that he'd get in too deep, too quickly, judging by the effect one kiss had on him. It was better to put a stop to things now before things went any further and ruined the life he was trying to build for himself.

'Yes. You're right. Better just to leave things as they are.' She was flustered now, pressing and pressing the button on the fob in a hurry to get the gates open again.

Ángelo hated that things had ended this way after such a good night. Now she couldn't seem to get away fast enough.

He waited until she disappeared into the villa and watched the gates slowly close between them again. The barrier he apparently needed between them at all times. Next time he went out for a drink and an impromptu karaoke session he should probably do it alone, or with a woman who wasn't a work colleague. If he was ready to get back on the dating scene he needed to set his sights on someone uncomplicated, someone who didn't have a lot of emotional baggage with the people who ran his work place. Preferably with someone who wanted the same things as he did. From everything he'd learned about Inés, he didn't think family was on her list of priorities. A red flag he needed to take heed of when he was setting up his life so he could have one of his own.

'Inés? Is that you?' Her mother peered out from her bedroom, no doubt disturbed by the sound of the electric gates clanging open and closed.

'Yes. Sorry if I woke you. Ángelo and I just stopped for a couple of drinks and got caught up in a medical emergency.' Inés was struggling to keep her voice calm when her head was in the clouds after kissing Ángelo. She felt as though she was floating on air and it was difficult to come back down to earth so quickly. Regardless that their passionate embrace had ended so abruptly.

'You two seem to be getting on well.' Her mother walked down towards the lounge to greet her, then made her way to the adjoining kitchen to pour herself a glass of water.

'We're a good team when it comes to work,' she admitted, hoping her flushed cheeks wouldn't give away the effect he really had on her.

'I know he's glad to have you on board as much as we are.' Her mother cleared her throat and took a sip of water. 'We haven't really had a chance to talk since you came back.'

'Well, there's been a lot to deal with.' She wasn't sure she was ready to have this talk. It was easier in some ways just to get on with her workload and put the past behind her, rather than deal with it head on. She didn't want any more arguments to arise when she had nowhere else to go.

'I just wanted to thank you for coming back. I know things haven't been easy between us.'

Inés shifted uncomfortably at the understatement, but held her tongue. Clearly, her mother wanted to get something off her chest.

'It must have taken a lot for you to come back

and it has made me think hard about what happened. In hindsight, I can see that I didn't support you enough. I'm aware how difficult your father can be and I found life was easier simply to let him get his own way. It wasn't fair to expect you to do the same.

'You're stronger than I ever was and I'm so proud of you, Inés. I just hope that you can forgive me and hopefully give me a chance to repair the damage.' It was obvious her mother had been doing some soul searching and it was more than Inés had ever expected to hear from either of her parents. The admission reached deep inside her heart to that place where she'd been holding out some hope of having a family again.

Though she didn't know if she would ever find the same sense of closure with her father, Inés found herself wanting to let go of the resentment she'd held towards her mother for so long. Life with Marty had taught her how much she needed someone in her life she could turn to. Someone she could trust.

'It's okay, Mama. I know what it's like to love someone who takes over your life so much you can't even think for yourself any more. My life in England wasn't as rosy as you might think. I ended up living with a man who tried to control everything I did. It's given me some understanding of what you went through. But I've left Marty and I'm here now. Hopefully, we can move on together.' Inés made the first step forward and opened her arms.

Her mother hugged her tight, as though afraid she'd never see her again. 'I hope so. I'm just glad you got out and made your way back home.'

Inés couldn't promise her that she would be here for ever, but hopefully they would have each other again for some time to come. She went to bed with her heart feeling very full for once.

Inés didn't know how she was going to look Ángelo in the eye this morning. Things last night had been…unexpected and left her dealing with all sorts of jumbled emotions. Not only had she had a much-needed heart-to-heart with her mother, but she'd had that kiss with Ángelo to think about all night. She hadn't realised how much one night out could have such an impact on her. Now she had to see him every day knowing the passion which had sparked so easily to life between them.

It was clear he regretted it the moment it had happened, but she couldn't say the same. That kiss had awakened something inside her that she couldn't seem to shut down again. So many thoughts had been running through her head since. Including how much time she'd wasted being with Marty. She didn't want to repeat past mistakes by being blinded by a handsome man showing her affection and attention. In her experience it didn't last.

It would be nice to be able to let herself get swept away in the romantic fantasy of being with Ángelo without worrying about the consequences, but life with Marty had been so stifling she couldn't take that risk. Ángelo was handsome, kind, successful and wanted to settle down. All the qualities anyone could need in a man. Everything she'd thought Marty was in the beginning, too.

There was no room in her life for any sort of relationship at present, even a casual one. Especially with Ángelo. She was only back in Spain because of her parents and getting involved with her father's employee would only complicate matters between them. Things were messy enough and she didn't need to be distracted by a pretty face and a pair of strong lips.

That was part of the problem now. By kissing her like that, Ángelo had made her wonder if she'd been missing out on that level of passion. Or if it was something only Ángelo could whip up inside her. It was probably just hormones and her sense of freedom which had made their encounter all the more exhilarating, and nothing more. Kissing someone who wasn't Marty felt as though her liberation was complete. Because she'd wanted to, not felt as though she had to. She was no longer bound to a life she didn't want, or couldn't escape.

Inés hadn't had a lot of experience with men before Marty. One or two short-lived flings, but she didn't remember ever getting carried away in the moment the way she had with Ángelo. If it felt like that every time a man touched her, perhaps she was missing out by remaining single after all. She just had to remember to be careful she didn't end up with another control freak again, or get involved with someone she knew she couldn't be with. Either way, she'd be the one who'd end up getting hurt.

Though she was sure her mother would be over the moon with the idea of her being with Ángelo. Her mother was clearly fond of him and she'd made no secret of the fact she wanted Inés to stay in Spain. Especially now that their mother/daughter relationship was beginning to heal. She'd already had to fend off a thousand questions this morning over breakfast about her night out with Ángelo. Though she had known better than to give anything away other than the fact they'd had a drink and a chat. If her mother had any hint of the kiss they'd shared outside the house, she'd already be making plans for the wedding.

Thank goodness one of them had their feet

firmly on the ground. Though she had no idea why Ángelo had kissed her in the first place if he wasn't interested in her that way. Most likely it had been drink fuelled. A lot of bad decisions were made under the influence of alcohol. She'd first kissed Marty at a bar after working a late shift together at the hospital and that hadn't turned out so well in the end...

All she did know was that Ángelo had got her all hot and bothered, then dropped her like a stale churro. She'd have been better off not knowing what it felt like being in his arms, or being kissed so passionately.

'Morning.' He passed by without a second glance, telling her all she needed to know about how he felt about their night together. Embarrassed.

'I hear you two had fun last night.' Inés's mother, unaware of any awkward tension between the pair, addressed them both as they passed through reception.

It stopped Ángelo in his tracks long enough to glare at Inés. She could only hope her wide-eyed, innocent expression conveyed to him the fact she hadn't told her mother anything about the kiss they'd shared.

'It was just a drink, Mama...' Inés did her best to play it down and let Ángelo know she hadn't spilled any of the juicy details.

'I think we needed it to decompress after a difficult day at work.' Ángelo offered her mother a smile as he helped to try to diffuse the situation.

Though her mother seemed determined to blow things up again.

'Inés seemed to have enjoyed it. She was certainly in a good mood this morning.' The mischief in her mother's eyes said she knew it had been more than alcohol which had Inés stumbling in late in a daze.

Inés gave an exaggerated tut and rolled her eyes at her mother, which proved effective when she walked away without pursuing the matter any further.

'Sorry about that,' Inés apologised to Ángelo for her mother's insistence on bringing up what was clearly a moment he wanted to forget. Even if it wasn't proving so easy for her.

'It's all right. I suppose it takes her mind off your father for a while thinking there's some great romance going on under her nose.' His smile this time didn't quite reach his eyes, suggesting that he hadn't been able to brush off the matter as easily as he would have her believe.

Clearly, kissing Inés wasn't something he wanted to be reminded of. Never mind the insinuation that there would ever be anything more than that between them.

128 SPANISH DOC TO HEAL HER

It gave Inés a sinking feeling in the pit of her stomach, but she told herself she would've felt the same way if anyone rejected her. Trying to convince herself it didn't hurt more because it was Ángelo who was doing the rejecting after a kiss which had rendered her a puddle of hormones.

'I know, right? As if.' Inés did her best to laugh off any hint of romance between them, trying to convince herself as much as Ángelo that she hadn't read too much into the kiss.

They were left staring at one another in awkward silence and it occurred to her that she might have been better off letting him walk past her as he'd intended.

'We had a good talk last night and I think we managed to clear the air. One down, one to go,' Inés joked, though she wasn't looking forward to the particular conversation she needed to have with her father.

'I'm so happy for you both.' Ángelo pulled her into an unexpected embrace. As though he'd been as anxious for them to resolve their differences as her mother clearly had.

Inés tensed, afraid that if she let herself get too comfortable in his arms, she'd never want to leave. He slowly released her and she took a step back.

'I should probably get on with some work—'

Ángelo said, looking concerned that he'd encouraged physical contact with her again.

'What have you got planned for today?' Inés stumbled over his excuse to leave with some small talk.

'Work,' he repeated.

'Oh, yeah. Me, too.' She nodded, hoping at some point either the ground would swallow her up, or there would be another crisis somewhere to divert their attention away from this exchange.

Goodness knew how they were going to keep working together when she couldn't seem to let go of what had happened last night.

'Oh, I was going to go and see your father this afternoon,' he added, as an afterthought, clearly not recognising how much his dismissal of their kiss had hurt her.

'Okay.' She wasn't sure what he expected her to say to that.

Well done? Good for you?

'You could go, too. I'm sure he'd like to see you, Inés. It might be easier for you if I was there with you when you saw him. I mean, I'd let you talk privately. I could just be there for moral support.'

Although she appreciated he was doing his best to facilitate a mediation between her and her father, it wasn't something she wanted to think about right now. 'I'm not getting into this again, Ángelo. I know you have family issues, but they're very different to mine. Please leave it alone.'

The frustration she'd been feeling not only about the change in dynamic between them, combined with his continued attempts to reconcile her with her father, manifested in her raising her voice at him. She wasn't proud of it, but neither was she going to stand back and let another man try to dictate her actions.

He held up his hands. 'I just thought since you'd made up with your mother that you'd welcome the chance with your father, too. That it might have been easier if I went with you. Sorry if I read the situation wrong. My bad.'

Her rage only increased as he walked away, but this time it was directed at herself. It wasn't Ángelo's fault he didn't want her, any more than he was to blame for her strained relationship with her father. She was beginning to think it was her own guilt which was making her defensive when it came to any conversation around her father.

He was dying and she felt that obligation to see him before he passed away. It was her own personal issues that were stopping her. Along with that anxiety that he wouldn't have changed and might still try to dominate her in some way. Ridiculous, she supposed, given her age and the time which had passed between them. She just didn't want to revert back to that submissive version of herself that she'd only just shaken off.

At some point she knew she would have to visit him. Before it was too late and she spent the rest of her life feeling guilty. She didn't want to give him that power over her again.

'How are you today?' Ángelo took a seat by Juan's bedside, careful to avoid the wires and machines monitoring his vital signs.

'Still dying,' he replied without a trace of humour. This was the man he'd come to know over the years. Straight to the point, not bothered whose feelings he might hurt.

Ángelo supposed at this point of his life he had every right to say exactly what he thought without any regard for anyone else. Though he was beginning to see the kind of father he'd likely been to Inés and understood her reluctance to get close to him again.

Ángelo's visit had been a last-minute decision, for various reasons. Not only had it been some time since he'd stopped by, but it had been a good excuse to get away from the clinic for a while. His decision to ask Inés along might have been misjudged, but he'd thought it was the nudge she'd needed to take that final leap.

She certainly seemed pleased to have a relationship with her mother again and he was sure by seeing her father she would get that same sense of closure. Even though suggesting that he accompany her had negated the idea of putting some space between them after last night and he'd managed to get Inés's back up at the same time.

He hadn't meant to push her into doing something she hadn't wanted to do, but he just wanted to see her happy. It was more of an olive branch after the way he'd acted post-kiss. As though in some way being with her when she visited the parent she'd been estranged from for a decade would make up for him kissing her, then telling her to forget it had ever happened. Now he'd managed to rile her twice over.

She seemed to have that effect on him—muddling his thoughts so he made some questionable decisions. Not that it was her fault. He'd been the one who'd instigated the kiss after all. Though her enthusiastic response had eventually been the catalyst for him to end it. He couldn't risk getting carried away any more than he already had been.

Now she probably thought that not only was he some kind of kiss-'em-and-leave-'em playboy, but someone who thought he could still get her to do things she didn't want to do. To some extent making him look like the same kind of control freak she was doing her best to stay away from.

Perhaps this visit was subconsciously some kind of atonement. Being charitable to her father to make amends for the mess he'd made with his daughter.

'Is there anything else they can give you to make you more comfortable?' It was difficult to know what to say in the circumstances. The man was dying, there was no point in denying that, and nothing he could say could change the inevitable.

Juan, whose usually trim figure was now bloated with fluid, could barely left his head from the pillow to 'tut' at him. 'More painkillers which don't do anything except make me sleep. Not that I can sleep very long with all the noise going on in here. If it's not the man next to me snoring, it's the nurses chatting to one another instead of doing their jobs.'

Ángelo had to suppress a smile that Juan still had the energy to complain even on his deathbed. He didn't envy those looking after him and no doubt hearing the same criticism. It reminded him all too much of the verbal, and sometimes physical, abuse he'd endured when taking care of his own father at the end of his life. At times it was very difficult to take when he was giving everything, sacrificing a life of his own, to look after someone who didn't seem to appreciate him.

He didn't blame Inés for being reluctant to visit, regardless that Juan's acting out was likely because he was scared and in pain. That's what he'd had to tell himself when his own father had been particularly vicious towards him, too. He certainly wouldn't want Inés to suffer the same kind of abuse and perhaps it was best for her own safety and sanity that she did stay away after all.

Not everything was as black and white as he'd once seen it. Having grown close to Inés these past few days, he could understand her position better and his brothers', to an extent. He'd been able to compartmentalise the things his father said and did from the care he'd needed, but that didn't make Ángelo a better person than anyone else. In hindsight now he could see how damaging that time could have been to his brothers if they'd been as affected by what had happened, as Inés clearly had been. He just wished there was some way that they could all find some kind of peace with the past that would allow them all to move on.

'There was a fire yesterday at the Garcia place. Inés and I were at the scene, but I think the couple are going to be okay. Some smoke inhalation and minor burns, but I was glad to have her with me.' He tried to make some small talk, at the same time trying to make Juan feel connected to the practice still and talk up Inés.

'Marie said she was home. I hope she's not giving you too much trouble.'

'Not at all. She's been great to work alongside.' The only trouble he'd had with Inés had been his own doing. Getting too close, too soon, then having to pull back before someone got hurt.

Professionally, she'd been a great addition to the practice and he enjoyed working with her. So much so he'd started to see something blossoming between them that they couldn't afford to nurture.

Juan didn't look impressed. He closed his eyes as though bored with the conversation, though Ángelo knew it was likely the morphine the medical staff had administered for his pain was making him sleepy.

Nevertheless, it didn't make it seem as though he was keen to make up with Inés even if she had turned up here with him, offering her sympathy and apologising for being away for so long.

'Always causing trouble,' he muttered, not opening his eyes.

It was a shame the two hadn't been able to put the past behind them to meet and get to know the people they were now. Before it was too late.

'Inés is an excellent doctor.' Ángelo felt the need to stick up for her in her absence. She hadn't done anything wrong since coming back. In fact, she'd helped out during a very difficult time for them all, when she really didn't have to.

Given the family history, she could very well have declined to come all this way and work at the practice, and no one would have blamed her. Well, except for her father.

'She hasn't come to see me.' This time, Juan sounded more emotional. More human. As though this was the matter that had really been bothering him.

'She's been busy with work. I'm sure she'll come at some point.' Ángelo didn't want to make any false promises, but he had a suspicion that Inés would make an appearance eventually. She was too kind hearted not to see her dying father one last time.

'I'm running out of time. I need to see her.' Juan's voice was weak. Broken. As though that gruff exterior had finally been dismantled and, faced with his own mortality, he'd finally realised what was important. Making peace with his daughter.

'I know,' Ángelo said softly.

Despite the plea, he didn't want to interfere. If he recounted Juan's request to Inés, she might think he was trying to manipulate her. He'd already made that mistake once too often. The decision had to be Inés's to see her father and hopefully she'd make it soon without any outside influence. He didn't want her to live with any regret when it was difficult enough grieving for a parent.

If Inés found some closure with her father, then she might move on and leave him to live his life without the danger of falling for his unsuitable co-worker.

CHAPTER SEVEN

'I'LL DO THE DISHES, Mama. You made dinner.'
Although they'd fallen into something of a routine with her mother cooking every night, Inés
didn't want to be a burden. Especially when
her mother was travelling so often to and from
the hospital, trying to spend as much time with
her husband as possible. Nor did she want to be
treated as though she was a visitor in her own
home. However temporary it might be.

'Nonsense. I like to keep busy. You sit down
and I'll get you a glass of wine.' Her mother ush-
ered her into the sitting room, ignoring all offers of help. Leaving Inés no choice but to put
her feet up.

She would have preferred to keep busy, too. To
take her mind off yet another flare up between
her and Ángelo this afternoon. It seemed there
was a fine line between passion and aggravation.
He managed to arouse very strong emotions in
her either way. She supposed it was good in a
way that she no longer felt the need to hide how

she felt. To be afraid of expressing herself in case she suffered the consequences. She knew he wouldn't do anything to harm her, even if he managed to rile her at times.

No doubt he thought he was doing the right thing by trying to push her and her father back together, but those were big decisions she had to make for herself now. She wasn't going to let anyone tell her what to do any more. Unfortunately for Ángelo, when she was around him she was no longer the timid mouse Marty had made her into, but a tiger lady who wasn't afraid to bite back.

The thought made her smile. She'd come a long way in such a short space of time and he was partly to thank for that when he gave her the space to express herself. No matter how ferociously at times.

The bell sounded at the gate and she rushed towards the front door to let in their visitor, keen to have a distraction. Only to see the gates open at her behest, revealing Ángelo standing there like a mirage. Her pulse immediately kicked up a notch as she remembered being in that very spot with him last night, with his lips on hers.

She gulped and swallowed down the carnal thoughts that sprang to mind, ready to greet him.

'Is Mama expecting you?' Her mother hadn't said anything, but this could be another arrangement she wasn't aware of. Or a misguided attempt at matchmaking, inviting Ángelo over as a post-dinner snack for her.

'No. Sorry. I hope I'm not disturbing you. Your father wants a few things brought up in the morning and I said I'd deliver the message to your mother.'

'No problem.' An unexpected surge of disappointment swelled inside her that he hadn't made a special trip just to see her. Regardless that they hadn't parted on the best of terms this afternoon.

Inés led him into the villa, regardless that he probably knew the place better than she did these days. She tried not to get too caught up in the feeling that he'd replaced her here, especially when he was the one visiting her dying father, too.

'How was he?' she asked, surprising them both. 'I suppose that's a stupid question in the circumstances.'

'He's understandably feeling low, though still alert enough to complain about the staff,' Ángelo said with a curt laugh. 'I'm sure he'd be pleased to know you care.'

Her initial reaction was to refute the allegation, but in the end, she couldn't. No matter how he'd acted, no matter how estranged they'd become, he was still her father and he was dying. She didn't want him to suffer. She simply wished things had been different. That they could have had a better relationship. But she knew wishing for the impossible was a futile exercise when she'd spent years longing for things in her life to be different. The only way change came about was when she made it happen.

She chose not to rise to the comment.

'Ángelo? You should have said you were coming. We could have set a place for you at dinner. There's still some left if you'd like me to heat it up for you?' Her mother bustled into the lounge to greet him, then disappeared into the kitchen just as quickly. Not giving him a chance to refuse the offer.

Inés exchanged a smile with him. 'Looks as though you're staying.'

'Sorry. I didn't mean to spoil your evening.'

'You didn't. At least I'll have someone to talk to, I guess. Mama can't seem to sit down long enough for a conversation.' It wasn't the evening she'd expected to be having, but Inés knew her mother needed to keep busy. She enjoyed having visitors to fuss over and likely had been at something of a loss when Inés had left home. Ángelo had filled that void for her and now, more than ever, she needed something to keep her busy. Given too long to think, the inevitable loss of her husband would surely sink in and devastate her.

Grief was something Inés would have to deal

with, too, but was something she wasn't ready to think about either.

They followed her mother to the kitchen. At least then Inés wouldn't be left trying to make conversation with Ángelo on her own. It never seemed to end well. Either with an argument, or a dizzying kiss. Both of which left her ruminating for hours on their interactions. One scenario leaving more of an impact on her than the other...

'Juan wants you to bring up some clean pyjamas and his razor.' Ángelo took a seat at the breakfast bar and watched as his hostess plated up some dinner for him.

'Still wanting to look his best.' Inés opened a bottle of wine and poured three glasses, before pulling over a tall stool to sit next to him.

'Your father takes great pride in his appearance. I find it a comfort that even now he's trying to make the effort to look his best.' Inés's mother had tears in her eyes as she set down the plates of food for them all to pick from.

It crossed Inés's mind that her father would look considerably different from the last time she'd seen him and, if her mother was finding the change in him difficult, she would have to prepare herself, too. If she decided to go and see him.

'He was tired, but I think he enjoyed the company. It probably gets boring, not to mention lonely, lying in that hospital bed.' Ángelo, who was happily munching away on the sardines and patatas bravas before him, didn't appear to have been making a dig at her. Yet Inés couldn't help but feel guilty that this virtual stranger was providing the support she couldn't bring herself to give. It wouldn't bother her so much if she didn't still care.

'I know he wants to come home, but he's not able to get around unaided now. I'm not capable of lifting him if he has another fall.' Her mother's throwaway comment chilled Inés. It was clear her father had a history of bad falls which she'd known nothing about, but she was sure Ángelo was aware of.

'You'll do yourself more injury if you try to do that again. We both nearly put our backs out the last time we had to lift him in the bathroom. He's in the best place, Marie.' Ángelo squeezed her mother's hand, confirming that there had been more going on than Inés had known.

That guilt that she hadn't been here to help was only overtaken by the shame she felt by the fact she'd been busy trying to keep Marty happy. Even if she'd known at the time she wouldn't have risked upsetting him by suggesting she needed to come home to help look after her father. Thank goodness Ángelo had been here to help. She would have hated to think of her mother having to deal with all of this on her own.

'I know. It's just not easy. I'll put a smile on my face and go and see him in the morning.' Her mother gave a heartbreaking wobbly smile, showing how vulnerable she was beneath the efficient exterior she tried to portray.

Despite everything Inés's father had put them through, it was clear her mother still loved him, and would likely be lost without him.

'Maybe you could take him some of that cheese you bought. It's delicious.' Inés wanted to contribute in some small way, without actually committing herself to anything, and thought perhaps some snacks would cheer him up. Her father had always been fond of his food.

Except her mother shook her head. 'He doesn't have much of an appetite any more. Finds it hard to keep food down.'

Clearly Inés knew nothing about her father any more and it was becoming more apparent to everyone. Including her.

Rather than discuss the matter any further, Marie de la Fuente began tidying up again. Carrying the empty glasses and dishes over to the sink, refusing all offers of assistance. She stood with her back to Inés and Ángelo for several moments and Inés thought she was just trying to compose herself.

Suddenly, she collapsed to the ground, and the glass which had been in her hand smashed all around her.

'Mama?'

'Marie?'

Both Inés and Ángelo immediately rushed over to see her. Although conscious, she was clearly dazed, and her hand was bleeding profusely.

'I just felt a little dizzy.' She tried to get up, but Ángelo placed a gentle hand on her shoulder.

'Stay where you are for now.' He went to fetch a glass of water and Inés began sweeping away the shards of broken glass around her so they could get down to take a better look at her.

'You've cut your hand.' Inés wadded it up with some paper towels before going in search of the first-aid kit she knew was kept in the bathroom cabinet.

When she came back, her mother was sipping from the glass of water, as Ángelo checked her pulse.

'Your heart's beating a little fast right now. It could just be from the shock of the fall, but I want you to stay where you are for now until we see if it regulates itself again.'

'How are you feeling, Mama? Light headed?

Dizzy? Any headache?' Inés, like Ángelo, wanted to get to the bottom of why she'd collapsed.

'A little lightheaded, I suppose. Everything just seemed to be so far away, then my head was spinning and the next thing I knew I was on the floor.' She was pale and suddenly looking her age, sitting there so vulnerable.

'It's no wonder when you're rushing around the way you have been. You need to rest, Mama, and look after yourself for once.' Inés carefully picked the tiny fragments of glass out of the cut across her palm, before cleaning the wound.

'Are you eating properly? You're so busy making sure everyone else is eating, but I'm sure I haven't seen you eat anything more than a nibble of food lately.' It was Ángelo's turn to scold her.

Hopefully, she didn't need anything other than some rest and a proper meal.

'I'm not really hungry. My stomach always seems to be in knots, thinking about Juan.' Goodness knew how she was going to cope when he was gone for good, but Inés was simply grateful that she'd come here when she had. Then she could look after her mother while they were under the same roof.

'You're under a lot of stress, Marie. Even more reason why you should be taking better care of yourself. I'm prescribing a couple of days off work to get some rest. I can take Juan's things to him.' Ángelo's stern, but concerned, tone wasn't one to be argued with.

'I can't ask you to do that and who's going to look after the clinic if I'm not there?' It appeared she wasn't going to go down without a fight.

'You didn't ask me. I offered. We can get agency workers in to help until you're ready to get back on your feet. Isn't that right, Inés?' Ángelo looked to Inés for support and, in this case, she was happy to give it.

'Yes. Mama, you're under too much stress, doing too much. You need to rest. I don't think this needs stitches, but you do need some sleep. We're going to help you to bed and I don't want to hear any complaints.' Inés didn't want to be dishing out tough love, but she needed her mother to comply. The last thing she wanted was another parent ending up in hospital. Especially when they'd just begun repairing their relationship. She didn't want to face the possibility of losing her, too.

Inés finished dressing the cut on her mother's hand and Ángelo checked her heart rate again. Once he was satisfied that she didn't need hospital intervention, he and Inés helped her mother to her feet.

'I suppose it wouldn't hurt to get an early night,' she finally conceded.

'And a lie in. I'll bring you breakfast in bed

before I go to work in the morning. I'm going to make sure you do everything your doctor tells you.' Inés smiled at Ángelo, safe in the knowledge they were both in agreement on this matter at least.

Escorting her with an arm each, they walked her mother to her bedroom, then left her to get ready for bed in private. Although Inés promised she'd come and check on her soon to make sure she actually got into bed and wasn't doing office paperwork, or something other than taking it easy.

'I'm sure she'll be okay,' Ángelo reassured her as they left her room. 'She's just been dealing with a lot lately.'

'I know. I think I forget sometimes that she's ten years older than the last time I saw her. I suppose you just think your parents are going to last for ever.' Inés supposed she had thought eventually that they would reconcile and never considered that it would be under these circumstances. When she was going to lose her father sooner rather than later and some day it was going to be her mother, too.

There was no hiding from that fact, try as she might, and she knew if she didn't reconcile with her father now, it could be too late. She might never get that closure she needed if she didn't see him. Even if she wasn't emotionally ready for that confrontation with her past.

'Until they aren't there…' Ángelo seemed to drift off into his own thoughts. He talked so little of his own family, Inés had forgotten he was probably missing them, too.

She headed straight back to the kitchen to grab what was left of the wine. Ángelo took two new glasses from the cupboard and they carried everything into the lounge.

'How long has it been since you lost your father?' Inés asked as they sat down. She kicked off her shoes and curled her legs under her, getting comfy.

'Five years.' Ángelo poured two generous glasses of red and handed one to her.

'You've been on your own all that time?' Yes, she was prying, but she wanted to know more about him when he was clearly such a big part of her parents' lives and knew so much about hers.

'Pretty much. My brothers don't get in touch very often.'

'Don't you get lonely?' She didn't believe someone as warm and loving as Ángelo obviously was wouldn't have someone beating on the door of the handsome doctor. After all, he'd managed to enchant her after only a few days of getting to know him.

He took a sip of wine and captured her with

his intense gaze. 'I'm not a monk, Inés. It's not as though I haven't shared a bed with anyone in five years.'

'Oh.' Inés felt her cheeks flush. She wasn't a prude, but the idea of him casually hooking up with random women to fulfil his carnal needs did make her blush. It also aroused a twinge of jealousy, when she'd been afforded a passionate kiss from him, but denied the rest of that pleasure.

'What about you? Surely there was someone back in England?' He was teasing her, but Inés found herself wanting to open up about Marty. She'd kept the details of the relationship secret for years, as though it was something she should be ashamed of. It had been a big part of her life. Made her who she was now and she wanted to exorcise herself of that particular demon so she could forget about him.

'I was in a long-term relationship up until recently.'

'It must have been difficult for you to leave and come back here. Is that what caused the break up?'

Inés inhaled a shaky breath. This was the moment she thought she'd never come to, when she opened up about what she'd been through. But Ángelo felt like a safe space. Hopefully he wouldn't blame, or shame, her for the circumstances she'd let herself get into.

'No, but it was a good reason for me to leave. I'm not sure I would've found the courage to do so otherwise.' She gulped her wine.

'That bad?' Ángelo's eyes were full of concern and it encouraged her to tell him everything and get it off her chest once and for all.

She nodded, willing the tears to stay at bay when she was trying to be strong. 'Not at first, of course. Marty was very charming and attentive when we met. I suppose I was naive. I hadn't been allowed to date here, so when I moved to London I was easily flattered by the attention I received. The men I dated turned out to be immature and only interested in partying. I thought Marty was different. He was older, a handsome, successful surgeon, and he had his own place in the city.'

'I can see why your head was turned. I might have dated him myself at that age.' Ángelo was trying to make her feel better about her choices, but they both knew he was more careful than that when it came to relationships.

'I rushed into things. Who knows, maybe I was just trying to find some stability in my life. I wanted the happy ever after, but it turned into a nightmare. Marty gradually took control of everything. Of me and my life. To the point where

I wasn't allowed to do anything without his say so. I was afraid to do anything in case it upset him. Basically, I swapped one control freak for another. So you see, I'm not the strong, independent woman you've mistaken me for.'

'You broke away, didn't you? I see no mistake.' He took a sip of wine and didn't bat an eyelid at her big reveal.

'I was weak.'

'You were conditioned, Inés. In some ways, so was I. We repeat the patterns we've grown up with. In your case it was having someone control you. With me, I couldn't let go of the fact my father was my family. Regardless of how he treated me. We're both survivors and probably better people for what we've come through. I don't suspect either of us would ever cause the same pain to anyone else that our parents caused us.'

It was an angle she'd never explored before. Ángelo's insight certainly gave her something to think about. She didn't see him as weak, or stupid, for looking after his father. Clearly, it wasn't how he saw her either.

'You're right about that. Nor will I ever again be with someone who tries to clip my wings. What about you? No horror dating stories?'

Ángelo swallowed his wine with a gulp and

she got the impression there was more to his story than a troubled childhood too.

'I was with someone for a couple of years. Camila. I thought we would settle down and raise a family.'

'And she didn't?'

He shook his head. 'We were young. I was still living with my father and studying medicine. In hindsight, I didn't have much to offer. She ended things when she realised I couldn't put her first. I suppose that helped spur me on to be a success, to have that stability in place that I never had as a child.'

Inés could tell he'd been hurt deeply by the rejection when he hadn't seemed to have had a serious relationship since. Believing that no one would have him unless he could provide them with material things.

'If she'd really loved you, she would've wanted to be with you no matter what. The right person wouldn't care how much you earned, or where you lived. You only hurt yourself by staying too long with the wrong person. I'm sure you'll find the right one some day.' Her heart ached at the fact that it wasn't going to be her.

Ángelo held her gaze. 'I hope so.'

Inés's heart started pounding loudly. They were sitting so close. He was so understanding. She was so lonely.

'I should get these dishes done before Mama insists on doing them herself.' There were only a couple of glasses and plates, but she needed to breathe some air which wasn't filled with Ángelo's spicy cologne.

She got up to take the glasses into the kitchen and put some distance between them, but her plan was thwarted when he followed her into the kitchen. Barefoot, she padded across the tiled floor, not thinking anything of it until she felt a sharp stabbing pain in the sole of her foot and cried out. She crumpled to the floor, with a concerned Ángelo standing over her.

'What's wrong?'

Showing off her flexibility, Inés managed to bring her foot up to inspect it and found the culprit. 'I've stood on a tiny sliver of broken glass. I must've missed it when I was sweeping up.'

Ángelo crouched down and inspected the puncture wound where the blood had begun to pool. 'We need to get that out before it disappears beneath the skin. Sit still.'

He grabbed the first-aid kit from earlier which had been left on the kitchen worktop and rummaged around inside. With a pair of tweezers, he held her foot in one hand and carefully extracted the glass. Inés watched the concentration on his face, thinking more about the warmth of his touch than her injury.

'Sorry for causing more drama.' It was second nature for her to apologise for virtually everything, but this one was on her. She should have cleaned up properly and should not have been walking about barefoot.

Ángelo frowned at her and her heart gave that extra beat it always used to do when she thought she'd upset Marty and was about to be subjected to one of his rages.

'You don't need to apologise for anything, Inés. It was an accident.'

'I should have been more thorough when I cleaned up. I'm lucky it wasn't Mama who stood on it.' She sat still while he cleaned the small wound and placed a plaster over the area.

His jaw clenched. 'Listen to me. These things happen. You're not going to be punished for a mistake. You're safe here.'

She had no idea she was still in victim mode until he'd pointed it out. He was right. She had become conditioned to always accepting blame. It was disturbing that even away from Marty's influence, she was still acting as though he had control over her. The frustration of that brought tears burning her eyes.

'I hate that he can still do this to me.'

'Don't let him,' Ángelo said softly. 'From now on you're free to do whatever you want, express however you feel. Without having to worry about the repercussions. At least with me.'

Inés wished that were true. Because she'd be acting on those very feelings right now when he was cradling her foot, being all thoughtful and looking as gorgeous as ever.

She pondered over that for a moment, saw the way he was looking at her, too, and threw caution to the wind. Inés leaned in, stroked his cheek with her palm and kissed him gently on the lips. When they broke apart, it seemed like for ever as she waited for his reaction. Then he yanked her leg, pulling her towards him, her backside sliding across the smooth tiles, until she was flush against him. Her legs wrapped around his hips.

Before she could even register what was happening, his mouth was crushing hers, passionate and demanding. She melted into him. This was exactly what she wanted and she wasn't going to let anyone take this moment away.

Ángelo knew he shouldn't be doing this, but how could he lecture Inés on not letting the voice of the past ruin her present when he was guilty of doing the same? Kissing Inés was what he wanted, but he kept letting old insecurities hold him back. As he'd told her, he wasn't a monk. He had needs and wants, and recently they were all wrapped up in her. They didn't have to promise each other for ever, but they could enjoy this for what it was without overthinking everything. It was clear they had chemistry and they couldn't fight it for ever. Perhaps it was about time they stopped living their lives without thinking about future consequences and simply enjoyed the moment.

Inés was straddling his lap now, her arms around her neck, her curves pressed tightly against his body, kissing him with a fervour which was setting his whole body on fire for her. He wanted her and the feeling was clearly mutual. So why deny themselves?

'What about your mother?' That was one reason they probably shouldn't get too carried away.

'She'll be out for the count now. She won't hear us.' Inés was kissing him all over, making his brain fuzzy and his body hard.

'Bedroom?' he asked, knowing exactly what was on both of their minds.

'First door on the right,' Inés mumbled into his neck between kisses.

With the last hurdle seemingly not a problem at all, Ángelo's restraint completely snapped. He didn't have to hold back any more. No more pretending he didn't want this to happen. This had all he'd been thinking about. He scooped her up and carried her the short distance to her room and closed the door tightly behind them. Shutting out the rest of the world, so all they had to think about was what they wanted to do to each other.

He stripped Inés's top over her head, revealing her full breasts encased in ivory satin. Ángelo cupped them in his hands, kissing the tanned globes, worshipping them with his mouth and tongue as he peeled away the underwear. Inés gasped when he caught her nipple, grazed it with his teeth and tugged until she was writhing against him.

He set her down on to the floor and helped her strip away the rest of her clothes until she was standing gloriously naked before him. Brave. Bold. And sexy as hell.

They stood facing one another and Inés began to unbutton his shirt. Her shaking hands giving away her nerves. Ángelo shrugged the half-opened shirt over his head and she covered his chest with her hands. Trailing her fingers over his torso, electrifying his skin everywhere she touched him. He sucked in a sharp breath when she undid his trousers and let them fall to the ground, along with the rest of his clothes.

Inés glanced up and down his body, biting her lip as she did so. Only increasing Ángelo's arousal. He took her in his arms and kissed her until she relaxed against him. Then he laid her down on the small bed a young Inés had likely only ever slept in alone.

He kissed her neck, her throat, her pert breasts, watching the pleasure on her face as he did so. The pride he took in seeing her so undone, spurring him on in his quest to completely unravel her. He drew his hand along her inner thigh and dipped a finger into her molten core, eliciting a gasp from her in response.

As he drew her nipple into his mouth, he slipped his finger inside her, feeling her wet heat beneath his touch. Teasing, pleasing, he increased the pace of his attentions until she was panting with anticipation. Then he felt her tighten around him, she lifted up off the bed, and tried to stifle the cry of her release with her head buried in his chest. He matched her satisfied grin.

'Was it good for you, too?'

She laughed. 'I didn't realise how much I needed that. Needed you.'

'You haven't had me yet.' Ángelo wiggled his eyebrows and made her laugh again, her body rubbing dangerously against his as she did so.

'What about contraception?'

He left her briefly to retrieve his wallet from his trousers and pulled out the emergency condom he kept there.

'I always come prepared,' he said, covering her body again with his.

He kissed her with renewed desire and positioned himself between her legs, thrusting when he was sure they were both ready. Inés's eyes flew open as she gasped and he waited for her to adjust to him before he moved again. She kissed him and, arms braced on either side of her, he began to rock his body to hers.

As he'd told her, sex wasn't something he denied himself, but there was definitely something different about being with Inés. She wasn't a meaningless encounter fuelled by lust, but someone he had a connection with. Not only did they see each other every day at work, but they'd shared a lot with each other about their pasts and the scars they'd been left with. That emotional connection only seemed to heighten his passion and arousal.

They both knew how it felt to be hurt, to be found wanting in some way. Tonight it was clear that they were enough for one another and that was a powerful aphrodisiac in itself.

Joining their bodies together, feeling that euphoria of physical satisfaction, made him forget all the pain of the past. He wanted to have this all the time. Wanted Inés all the time.

With every thrust of his hips he brought them closer and closer to that final burst of bliss. Her little groans of pleasure urging him harder, faster, until all he could hear was the rush of blood in his ears. Everything in his body attuned to reaching that ultimate release for both of them. Ángelo wanted Inés to feel as good as he did. It had been hard to listen to how her ex had treated her, knowing this beautiful, strong woman deserved so much more. Even if it was just for one night he wanted her to be worshipped the way she always should have been.

'Ángelo—' When she gasped his name he was completely undone, barely holding back his needs until he knew for sure she was equally as satisfied.

Then her breathing changed into rapid pants, a whimper, her body contracting around his and the rush of her orgasm enveloping them both. Ángelo finally allowed himself to give in to his own pleasure, roaring his release into the crook of Inés's neck.

He was happy, he was exhausted, and he knew in that moment everything between them had changed for ever.

CHAPTER EIGHT

FIGHTING TO GET her breath back and regain control of both her brain and her body, Inés was stuck under the weight of Ángelo's body. And there was nowhere else she would rather be. Except somewhere they would have had more time and privacy to recover from their exertions without worrying about her mother discovering them. There was nothing she would have liked more than to simply curl up beside him for the rest of the night and let this fantasy play out a little longer.

Neither of them had anticipated this happening tonight, but it had probably been on the cards for a while. The kind of passion they'd shared was never going to have stayed bottled up for long. Instead, it had coming fizzing to the surface and exploded everything around her.

Ángelo, too, was panting, wiped out by the energetic, unexpected and extremely erotic encounter. Unfortunately they couldn't chance lying here naked any longer. They'd already taken a risk, blinded by desire. Now common sense had kicked in, the implications of being caught like this were too great to ignore a second longer.

'I don't know how we're going to explain this away if my mother catches us.' Despite current appearances, there was no way she was going to let her mother get carried away with the idea that they were going to be a couple. Inés didn't know what the future held, but she was sure that wasn't in their plans. Apart from anything else, she wasn't going to be railroaded into anything she wasn't ready for.

'I know. Just give me a second.' Ángelo didn't make any attempt to move as he mumbled against her neck, making her laugh.

'I'm serious. I don't want to feel like some shamed horny teen. We took the risk and got away with it until now. Let's not spoil things.' Though it was inevitable. Once they left this little bubble, reality would kick in, along with common sense, and they'd both try to distance themselves from what had just happened.

The only thing worse than trying to forget, would be her mother there to constantly remind her. Inés didn't need that when she was always going to have her own memory, along with the way her body reacted to him every time she saw him, to remind her of what they'd shared.

164   SPANISH DOC TO HEAL HER

'Okay.' He stirred momentarily, then flopped back down.

'Ángelo.' She slapped his back, trying not to laugh and encourage him to stay where he was. It would be easy to simply give in to the urge to stay here for as long as possible, but she'd learned not to jump into relationships. If they stayed here much longer, she had a feeling they'd end up drifting into one and she wasn't ready for that. Ángelo wanted a wife, children, a family. She needed to explore her independence before she even thought of that kind of serious commitment.

A groan, a shift of position, and Ángelo finally moved away. Inés immediately felt the loss. Not only of his body heat, but also of the connection they'd had. That moment when they'd been the only two people in the world, totally lost in the feelings they'd aroused in one another, was gone. Probably for ever. There was a certain kind of grief washing over her naked body at the realisation. Sadder still, as they dressed in silence.

'Do you want me to go?' Ángelo asked, as he put his shoes on.

'Yes. Sorry. I don't mean to sound harsh, but I don't relish the idea of sharing an awkward post-sex breakfast with my mother.' There were more reasons than that to put some distance between them, but this was one that would keep things simple between them. He didn't need to know she was afraid of getting too close, too quickly, and living to regret it as she had with Marty. Something told her he wouldn't appreciate being likened to her manipulative ex.

'No problem.' He made his way hastily to the door, probably relieved that she wasn't going to read too much into the fact they'd had sex. It had been obvious how much he'd regretted their kiss, so sleeping together was bound to give him heart palpitations once reality set in.

They both knew she wasn't the wife and mother he'd pictured when he'd been putting everything into place for his future family. This was a one off. A much-needed release which would hopefully put an end to the fizzing chemistry that kept testing her vow not to get involved with anyone for a long time to come.

He kissed her hard on the mouth, almost knocking her off her feet with surprise so that he had to sling an arm around her waist to keep her upright. Pulling her close to him and jump-starting all of those feelings that got her into trouble in the first place. The taste, smell and feel of him so very moreish she was tempted to forget those red flags all over again. Especially when the rewards were so great.

Although they'd had such a short time together, wary to some degree that they weren't alone in the villa, Inés had experienced an awakening. Sex with Ángelo hadn't been something expected of her, or that she'd felt obliged to engage in to avoid an argument or ill feeling. It had been an expression of her passion and desire, too. A feeling of freedom in simply doing as she pleased, giving in to those urges, and to hell with the consequences. As long as it never happened again and put her in danger of making more mistakes.

'Next time we'll got to my place where there's no worry about being interrupted.' Ángelo gave her a wink and walked away.

Devastating her attempt to convince herself this wasn't going to happen again. Because right now all she wanted was a repeat performance. Somewhere private where they had the freedom to explore one another completely for as long as they wanted. Where the new Inés had the same control of what happened in the bedroom as in every other part of her life. Denying herself the pleasure of sleeping with Ángelo again was letting Marty still have control, wasn't it?

By the time Ángelo had disappeared out of sight and Inés was closing the door, she was already planning on buying herself some new sexy underwear for their next rendezvous.

Sex didn't have to mean a serious commitment, or a lifetime of handing over control. It could just be having fun, exploring and enjoying a passion she'd never felt before. If she told herself that sleeping with Ángelo was simply another facet of her life as an independent woman, then she didn't have to worry about getting trapped with a man who wanted to change everything about her. She could walk away at any moment. Couldn't she?

It was the first time Ángelo was heading into work with knots in his stomach. A fluttering inside which grew faster and made him more nauseous with every step closer to work. Rising early and unable to even eat breakfast, he'd chosen to go on foot rather than by bicycle. Partly so he could have time to think, but also in case he caused an accident when he was so distracted.

He had no idea what he was facing this morning, or how he even felt about last night with Inés. The sex had been amazing. Passionate, powerful and all consuming. It was the implications of what they'd shared which had caused him concern. He knew there was no future for them as a couple, yet he wanted to do it all over again. Something he'd let her know as he left.

Now he had to face her in the cold light of day he'd find if it was something she was interested in, or would rather forget all about. He knew which one he'd prefer, otherwise it was

SPANISH DOC TO HEAL HER

going to make life very difficult at work. Seeing her, working with her and knowing how it felt to be with her.

Though getting romantically involved would bring its own problems, too, when she wasn't guaranteed to be in his life permanently. They both had some decisions to make—if last night was anything to go by, their libidos were leading the way instead of their heads.

The door to the clinic was already open when he got there, with Inés inside talking to the woman the agency had sent to cover her mother's absence.

'Morning.' He hovered in reception, waiting for some sign of how she felt about last night.

Her bright smile was a good sign. 'Morning. This is Giselle. I'm just giving her a rundown of how the place works.'

'Hello. I'm Ángelo.' He shook hands with the middle-aged blonde woman he was hoping wouldn't be around too long. As much as he wanted Marie to have a rest, he was looking forward to having her back so the place felt normal again. Regardless that things between him and Inés were now very different.

'I'll come and see you in your office once we're set up here.' Inés let him know her plan and he headed to his office with anticipation swirling in his belly.

There was no way of knowing what her decision would be regarding continuing what they'd started last night, but he was simply looking forward to spending time alone with her again.

When the brief knock came on his door he could stop pretending he was focusing on the paperwork on his desk. 'Come in.'

'Hey.' Inés entered, closing the door behind her, but not moving away from it to come closer to him.

'How's your mother today?' He thought they needed an ice breaker before they got to the serious stuff. Besides, he was genuinely concerned for both of her parents.

'I took her breakfast in bed and she's under strict instructions not to do anything strenuous. I think she just needs some rest.'

'Good. Oh, I took some stuff to the hospital for your dad and left it with the staff.'

'Thanks for that. At least that will put Mama's mind at ease that he got what he was looking for.'

'Yes. All under control.' Unlike his current emotions.

'So...'

'So...' He echoed her foray towards the elephant in the room, exchanging coy grins with one another over their shared secret.

'About last night...'

'Hmm?' It seemed she was as unsure of the next move as he was and he couldn't resist teasing her a little bit.

He watched her eyes sparkle and her cheeks redden. 'Don't make me spell it out.'

Unable to keep up the charade, or resist her any longer, Ángelo got up from his office chair and walked towards her. She bit her lip as she waited for him to come to her and telling him everything he needed to know about how she felt.

Ángelo brushed the soft curls away from her face so he could study her closer. 'You're so beautiful.'

The words slipped easily from his lips when he was this close to her, seeing her pupils dilate and her teeth worry her full lips. Whatever spell she'd cast over him was clearly still working when he was casting aside all of those doubts he'd fretted about this morning in favour of giving in to temptation all over again.

Then she tilted her chin up and drew him towards those lips he'd been dreaming about all night. He gripped her arms and kissed her hard, as though he was fighting the attraction and succumbing to it all at the same time. When he was with Inés it felt as though he had no control over his body, or his mind. Exactly what made her so dangerous. He didn't want to fall for someone who didn't have the same vision for the future as he did. Not when he'd been there before and still bore the scars.

Yet it seemed as though he was doomed to repeat the mistake when Inés was all he wanted in this moment.

Hands wound in her hair now, he drank her in. Sipping from her lips and savouring her sweetness. Inés draped herself around his body and it was clear that she was in as much trouble as he was.

Then the sound of patients congregating in reception, chatting to their temp, filtered through their passionate haze. Reminding Ángelo they both had jobs to do and his career was something he couldn't afford to be distracted from.

He gave her one last kiss before he took a step back so he could think clearly again. 'The clinic is open.'

'Right. Yes. We have work to do.' Inés sounded uncharacteristically flustered. She brushed down her clothes and patted down her hair where Ángelo's fingers had been entwined in her soft tresses.

'We can pick this up again later if you'd like?' He wasn't ready to put a permanent end to things just yet.

'I'd like.' Her smile made him want to take her back in his arms and forget work even existed.

'I have a couple of errands to run, so it might have to be a late one. Unless you'd like to come with me?' He hadn't expected to invite her into another area of his life he didn't usually share with anyone, but he wanted to spend more time with her. Even if it meant opening up even more to someone he knew was probably all wrong for him.

'I'd like.' Inés's agreement seemed to stun them both into silence. It was a knock on the door from his first patient which spurred them back into action, both going their separate ways to concentrate on the job at hand.

The end of the day couldn't come quick enough for Ángelo.

'I thought you didn't drive?' Inés wasn't sure whether to be impressed or horrified when Ángelo turned up outside the family home in a battered old van.

'I don't drive. It doesn't mean I can't drive. I've borrowed this to transport some things. That's why I told you to put something old on. In case you get dirty.' He leaned out the window and waved her round to the other side of the van.

Inés was beginning to wonder about her clothing choice now. When he'd told her he'd pick her up, and for her to wear old clothes, she thought it was just his way of telling her they weren't going anywhere fancy. Still wanting to make a good impression, she'd donned a floral embroidered, white linen shirt with her jeans. As she climbed into the van and saw the stack of bags and boxes in the back, she suspected it wasn't the correct attire for manual labour.

'So where are we going?' She noted his holey charcoal-grey T-shirt and faded jeans frayed at the knees and found it just as arousing as his pristine work wear.

It was another side to him. More in keeping with the wild side he'd shown last night in the throes of passion. Rough and rugged, and extremely sexy.

She had to give herself a mental shake. If they were going to sleep together tonight, it would be a long way off. After he completed whatever task apparently took priority over everything else. She was going to have to learn to keep her libido in check if she was ever going to survive whatever this was between them. It wouldn't do her any favours to lose herself in either the romance, or sex, and fail to keep herself protected a second time.

'To see a few friends of mine. I do some fundraising from time to time to get them some supplies.' Ángelo was doing his best to keep her in the dark, but Inés had a feeling she was about to see a whole other side to him. He had a habit of surprising her.

'I'm sure they appreciate it.' She had no idea

who these friends were, but the fact that he took time out of his work schedule to help them said they were important to him.

They drove in comfortable silence down the motorway before he turned off down a dusty track. A large white building came into view and Ángelo pulled up around the back.

'Okay. So, I need you to know before we go in...this is a shelter for victims of domestic abuse. I know you'll be discreet and compassionate, but some of the people here will be wary of you until they get to know you.'

She shouldn't have been shocked by the revelation given what she knew about his background, and his kindness, but she felt a wave of affection towards him for doing this. For being there for people who otherwise did not have any support. She was lucky she'd never experienced physical violence in the home, but she knew how it felt to be alone and not have anyone to turn to. Being unhappy at home was an awful position to be in and it took a lot of courage to walk away from the situation. As Ángelo kept telling her...

'Of course. Just tell me what you want me to do.' She didn't want to upset anyone, including Ángelo, but she was glad she had the opportunity to help, too, in some way. To assist someone who'd struggled to leave a toxic relationship as she had and simply needed some reassurance that things would work out.

'I have some toiletries and essentials to hand out, but if anyone needs a medical check, perhaps you could help? Some of the residents are naturally hesitant to leave the place to seek medical treatment and wary of a man coming into the building at all. Most of them know me and I've built up enough trust to engage with them, but the most recent inhabitants might prefer to deal with a woman.'

'I completely understand. Though if you'd told me I would have brought my medical bag,' she chided him, wondering if he'd been afraid to tell her all the details in case she declined the opportunity to attend with him.

'No problem. I've got plenty of medical supplies in the back, too.' He jumped out, opened her door for her, then unlocked the back door.

The scale of his fundraising efforts immediately became apparent, with the boxes stacked floor to ceiling. In typical Ángelo fashion, he'd downplayed the strength of his conviction to help these people.

'How did you fund all of this?'

Ángelo shrugged, then began lifting boxes out on to the ground. She couldn't help but stare, mesmerised by the flex of his biceps. Made all the more attractive by his altruistic gesture she

176   SPANISH DOC TO HEAL HER

was sure everyone beyond this place was oblivious to. She was certain if her parents had known she would definitely have heard them singing his praises for it.

The fact he did all this without the expectation of praise, and simply because he wanted to, wasn't helping her keep those emotional defences in place. Inviting her here to be a part of it should have set off alarm bells that this was already going beyond the casual relationship she told herself they were venturing into, but her inner swooning romantic didn't want to hear them.

'The usual...sponsored cycles, begging businesses to help, shaking a charity tin in every establishment within a hundred kilometres. It's not just me contributing. The whole community has helped make this happen.' Though not without a nudge from Ángelo.

'*Hola*, Ángelo!' A woman Inés guessed to be in her fifties, dressed in a polka dot jumpsuit and sporting a pink pixie haircut, greeted him with a kiss on each cheek.

She was irrationally jealous by the display until Ángelo introduced her and the woman displayed the same affection to her, too. Daniela apparently ran the shelter and called the others out from the house to help. One by one, anxious faces appeared at the windows and doors, making sure it was safe to come out before setting foot over the doorstep.

Inés couldn't blame them. For the first few days after she'd left Marty, she'd expected him to turn up. Jumping at every knock on the door, looking inside every car that passed in case he was watching her. There was a certain level of paranoia which followed long after that kind of relationship ended. She didn't know if she'd been more afraid of him making a scene and forcing her to go back with him, or that she'd convince herself he was the only person in her life that loved her. That perhaps she would be better off staying with him. Thankfully, coming out here gave her that space to realise she'd made the right decision in leaving.

'Take the boxes into the front room and we'll sort the distribution from there.' Daniela organised the troops, with Ángelo and Inés following the conga line all carrying boxes.

It wasn't long before they'd emptied the van and the front room of the house looked like a budget Santa's grotto. Though those in receipt of the basic supplies were every bit as overjoyed as a child on Christmas morning.

'It's funny how much the little things can mean when you have nothing.' Ángelo was standing beside her, watching the residents clutching on to

178 SPANISH DOC TO HEAL HER

bars of soap and bottles of shampoo, as though they were precious jewels.

'I suppose I was fortunate in that way when I had my income at least to buy the essentials after I left Marty.' If she'd given up her job, there was no way she would ever have been able to get away from him. Perhaps that had been his plan.

'A lot of these women leave with nothing. They're lucky just to get away with their lives in some cases.'

It made this set up all the more remarkable. That these women had somewhere to go knowing they would receive this help when they had nothing. It enabled them to take that giant leap and make the break. She was sure the children would be grateful for it, their haunted faces telling of the horror they'd gone through just to get here. Hopefully they'd find some peace here, as well as having a new future to look forward to.

'I don't think we'd be able to take in as many women if Ángelo wasn't on board. The donations mean we don't have to divert funds into basic essentials and can focus on supporting our residents.' Daniela sang Ángelo's praises for him, highlighting exactly how much his contribution meant to the shelter.

He flushed pink, clearly not used to receiving such effusive gratitude. 'Speaking of which, Inés is a doctor, too. We thought we could both offer our services today if anyone needs us?'

Although he was clearly trying to divert attention away from himself, Inés was keen to do something equally useful to the people here. 'Yes, I'm on hand for any medical queries. Just point me in the right direction.'

'I have a new mother and son who just arrived. They're still in their room, but I think they've had a particularly tough time, if you wouldn't mind having a chat with them? I think they're both harbouring some superficial injuries, but they weren't willing to go to the hospital when they first arrived.'

Inés and Ángelo agreed to see them and followed Daniela to a small room at the top of the stairs.

Daniela knocked on the door and went into the room first to make sure the new arrivals were comfortable speaking to them. Once they got the go ahead, they ventured into the darkened room.

'Hi. I'm Ángelo. I'm a doctor. Is it okay if I open the curtains so we can see a little better in here?' Ángelo's soft tone came across as nonthreatening and the woman huddled up to her small son nodded. Though she kept her wide eyes on him at all times as he let some light into the room.

'I'm Inés. I'm a doctor, too. Daniela said you

might need some medical treatment? We're here to help.'

The woman was watching Ángelo with some suspicion. Unsurprising if she'd been a victim of domestic abuse and saw men as a potential threat. Inés could relate to some extent when she was still wary of getting too close to anyone who might hurt her again too. Albeit in a different way.

When there was no response, she tried again. 'What's your name?'

'Sofia. This is Emiliano.' The woman stroked her son's hair as he huddled close. It was clear they were afraid to be separated, but Inés and Ángelo needed to assess them properly.

'Well, Sofia, if it's okay with you we want to give you both a check over? Ángelo could take a look at your son over there. We don't have to leave the room.' When Inés left Marty she only had herself to worry about. She could understand the woman's reluctance to let her son out of her sight when she was responsible for his safety, too. It was important that they didn't make them feel any more afraid than they already were so they knew they were safe here.

'Why don't you take a seat over here, Emiliano, and we can have a chat?' Ángelo patted the mattress on the other single bed across the room.

The boy looked at his mother for permission and she nodded, bringing a sigh of relief to Inés.

'I understand you've had a difficult time. I'm just here to help you, okay? Can you show me where you're hurt?' The woman cast an eye over to where her son and Ángelo were chatting about football. Once she was sure he wasn't watching, she carefully lifted her shirt at the side. Revealing very vivid purple bruising.

The sight made Inés clench her jaw in anger at the man who'd inflicted such awful injuries, but held her tongue.

'I'm just going to have a feel to make sure there's nothing broken. I'll be as careful as I can. Just let me know where it hurts.' Inés positioned herself so she was blocking the child's view and kept her voice low so he wouldn't hear their conversation.

She carefully felt around the injury, felt the woman tense and suck in a sharp breath.

'Sorry. I don't think anything's broken, but your ribs are very badly bruised. I'm going to sound your chest so this might be a bit cold.' Inés pulled out the stethoscope from Ángelo's medical bag and breathed on the end of it to try to heat it before positioning it under the woman's shirt.

If she had missed a rib fracture there was a possibility of it puncturing a lung, but everything sounded clear. It was just going to be painful for a while.

'You need to rest and give the bruising time to heal. I'll leave you some painkillers. Is there anything else you want me to take a look at?' Inés didn't want to cross any boundaries, and would only treat any injuries Sofia was comfortable sharing with her.

The woman parted her hair to reveal a gash at her temple. Blood had congealed in her hair, and it had obviously been a traumatic injury.

'Have you experienced any headaches, dizziness or nausea?' Inés didn't know exactly what had happened, but if she'd had a significant impact there was a possibility of concussion or worse.

Sofia shook her head.

'I'd prefer you to have it checked at the hospital. Promise me if you develop any of those symptoms you'll go immediately to A&E.' Inés didn't like to leave her here unchecked, but she was also aware the woman wasn't actually her patient. She could only advise and ask Daniela to keep an eye on her.

'I promise,' Sofia said meekly.

Inés's heart went out to the woman. She'd been through such a horrendous event and had no idea what the future held for her or her son. That level of uncertainty was stress in itself without the constant fear of her abusive ex turning up again. All she really wanted to do was give the woman a hug.

Instead she asked her to accompany her to the bathroom so she could get the wound properly cleaned.

She filled the sink with warm water and took some cotton pads and began to clean the area, wiping away the blood and grime. It took a lot to prevent a sob escaping not only for this woman and her child, but for the same scared Inés who'd been through something similar.

'Everything will be okay, you know. I know it might not seem like it right now, when everything is so frightening and overwhelming, but you have good support here.'

Sofia nodded, tears silently dripping down her cheeks. Even that was something she recognised, crying without making a sound. Doing it somewhere Marty wouldn't see or hear in case she incurred his temper. He hadn't had to use his fists on her when words had always been enough to control her. That thought that she was only lovable if she did as she was told. Not enough for her parents, or her partner, just the way she was. It dawned on her that so far, Ángelo hadn't asked her to change. Even when she'd been rude and abrupt to him, he hadn't chastised her. He accepted her, faults and all.

'I was in a bad relationship myself until recently.' Inés's words caused the woman to look at her with wide eyes.

'But you're a doctor.'

'I'm still human. Still capable of falling for the wrong man. I know how it feels to be trapped in a toxic relationship. You keep telling yourself that they'll change, or that you'll be better so you don't anger them. But it's not you and it wasn't me.' She took Sofia gently by the shoulders, wishing someone had given her this talk when she'd first made the break. It had taken her a while to understand she wasn't the one at fault.

'No...' Sofia said softly. 'I didn't hurt anyone. I had to protect my son.'

'Exactly. You've done the right thing for you and Emiliano. This is the start of your new life.'

A knock on the bathroom door interrupted their heart to heart.

'Inés? Is everything all right? Emiliano was getting worried about his mother.' Ángelo sounded concerned, too, and she realised she'd broken her promise not to leave the room.

Inés opened the door. 'I was just dressing a cut on Sofia's head.'

Ángelo hovered as she covered the wound with some paper stitches and a dressing and Emiliano was standing behind him.

'See, your mother's fine.' Ángelo moved aside so he could see for himself.

'Everything's okay. We're going to be okay,' Sofia said through a watery smile, giving Inés hope that her talk had helped in some way. It wasn't easy opening up about her own experiences, but it was important she knew she wasn't on her own.

'Well, Emiliano is fighting fit. He has a few scrapes and bruises, but nothing he won't shake off.' Ángelo and the boy exchanged a high five, with Emiliano already looking brighter and happier.

It occurred to Inés that the two might have shared a similar conversation. After all, Ángelo had been brought up in a similar environment and seeing the man he'd become would surely make him a positive role model for anyone.

'If there's anything you need, I'm sure Daniela has our contact details. I think you and Emiliano should both have counselling to help you move on. You've been through a lot. We can help you access whatever services you need.' Inés didn't want to overwhelm them all at once. The next steps should be down to Sofia, but she wanted her to know there were resources available for her.

'Yes. Anything you or Emiliano need, don't hesitate to get in touch. We want to get you back

SPANISH DOC TO HEAL HER

on your feet as soon as possible.' Ángelo held out his hand and Sofia shook it.

'Thank you both,' she said quietly, folding her son back in the safety of her arms.

Inés suddenly had to get out before she burst into loud messy tears and caused a scene, making them all uncomfortable. It so easily could've been her in this situation if she'd waited any longer to leave. If they'd had a child, he or she would've been subjected to the same life, or worse.

She *was* brave and so was Sofia.

'We'll see you again soon,' Ángelo promised as he hurried Inés out the door and out of the building.

He'd seen the wobble in her usually strong countenance and knew he had to get her out of the very emotive situation. They'd done everything they had to do and now he had to make sure she was okay.

He called their goodbyes and helped Inés into the van. Leaving a trail of dust as he drove away at speed, wanting to put some space between them and the shelter. Once he thought they were a safe distance away, he abruptly pulled the van over to the side of the road, undid his seat belt, and reached over to hug her tight.

'I'm so sorry. I should have realised it was

too soon to put you through that.' He'd only been thinking about what an asset she would be. Never imagining the horrors that were going on behind her strong exterior.

He'd overheard her in the bathroom sharing something of her experiences with Sofia. It was clear the relationship had been traumatic and still had a lasting impact on her, but she'd been so brave it was easy to forget how fragile she still was. And no wonder. It said a lot about her strength of character that she'd been able to come out here and work so soon. Especially to help her parents who she'd had a troubled relationship with, too.

It was about time someone took care of her for a change.

'It's okay,' she mumbled into his chest. 'I didn't expect to get so emotional either. It was just the thought of how I could have ended up, too. If I'd stayed. If we'd had children.'

Ángelo let go of her so he could tilt her chin up to face him. 'But you didn't. You were strong. You left. You're the bravest woman I've ever met.'

'Take me home,' she said firmly.

'Okay. I'm sorry. I shouldn't have brought you here. I'll take you home.' He buckled his seatbelt and started the van, sorry that he'd put her through this when he'd simply intended to share a part of his life with her he thought she'd relate to. Far too well it turned out.

Inés turned to him, jaw set with determination. 'No. I meant take me to your home.'

Ángelo hit the brakes. 'What do you mean?'

'You know what I mean. Tonight has reminded me that I wasn't to blame for what happened to me and I shouldn't let Marty dictate my life any more. I want to be with you, Ángelo, and I don't want my past stopping me from being happy.' She was back to being the direct Inés he knew, but he didn't want to take advantage of her when he knew she was emotionally vulnerable.

'As much as I want that, too, Inés, perhaps you need some space before you make any rash decisions you might come to regret.'

'Please don't tell me what I need. I've had enough of that for one lifetime. Unless you don't want me...'

Ángelo hated that he'd caused that little waver in her new-found confidence and reached out to grab her hand. 'Of course I do. I just want you to be sure it's what you want.'

Inés fixed him with those intense blue eyes. 'It is.'

With the strength of her response, there was no denying that going home with him was exactly what she wanted. He'd hoped that was where they'd end up tonight, Inés was simply taking the lead. Something he understood she needed to do after everything she'd been through.

Now the pressure was on Ángelo to make sure it wasn't something she'd come to regret.

CHAPTER NINE

INÉS'S BRAVADO WAS gradually ebbing away, the closer they got to Ángelo's place. When he pulled up outside his modest villa, her heart was pounding so loudly she was sure he'd be able to hear it too.

'Nice place,' she said, admiring the ochre-coloured, one-storey building with white-shuttered windows and roof terrace.

'Thanks. It's home. And I'm hoping I'll never have to move again.' He opened the gates and drove into the small driveway at the side of the house. With the gates closed again, and the high surrounding walls, it gave that feeling of being in their own bubble again. Of safety.

Inés tried not to think about the fact he'd probably bought the place with the idea of raising a family in mind. This was a home for someone intent on settling down with a wife and children. A long-term commitment with an eye on the future. Not a casual fling with someone who wasn't sure where she would be in a few months' time.

She fought the doubt demons threatening to spoil the evening and tried to recapture the warrior spirit which had brought her here in the first place. The Inés who knew exactly who and what she wanted and wasn't going to let anyone take it away from her.

There was tension in the air as they made their way inside. Anticipation for the evening ahead bouncing off the whitewashed walls. For a bachelor pad, it was well furnished—for comfort rather than aesthetic—with oversized sofas and plump cushions. The open-plan layout let her see the modern kitchen with the farmhouse-style dining room table dominating the room. All set up for the family he was expecting to have in the near future, no doubt.

She consoled herself with the fact that he'd known about her issues before they'd gone to bed together the first time. He'd been well aware of the sort of person she was, so she wasn't under pressure to pretend to be someone she wasn't. They'd both apparently decided that they still wanted a casual sexual relationship for whatever time they'd have together. Because she wasn't promising either of them any more than that. Even if she was beginning to long for more.

At this moment in time she was questioning her plans to leave as soon as possible. She couldn't imagine going now and never seeing Ángelo again. Although the idea of getting into another relationship terrified her, the future he'd painted for himself with a partner and children was bringing out the green-eyed monster inside her for the woman who'd get to share that with him. If she was brave enough, perhaps there was a chance to have that for herself.

'I had hoped to have my own home some day, too.' Inés had never really had the chance of living independently. She'd left her father's home and rules, flat shared for a while in London, then moved into Marty's place.

Although her parents' villa was home for now, it was really only because of her financial circumstances. Once she'd put enough money by, she'd hoped she'd be able to rent a small place. Not caring where, or what it looked like, as long as it was hers and she didn't have to rely on anyone else to have a place to stay. Now, being here with Ángelo, she wasn't sure that was still what she wanted. She'd been frightened to want more. Trying to protect herself from getting hurt again by isolating herself. But, if Ángelo was the man she thought he was, running away from her feelings could mean she was punishing herself by denying them a chance to be together.

Ángelo Caballero had well and truly stuffed up her plans for a quick getaway.

'It took a while for me to get to this point in my life and a lot of hard work. There's no feeling like it, though.' Ángelo looked understandably pleased with himself and Inés hoped that somewhere down the line she could be proud of herself, too. So far, she didn't think she'd done a lot to cover herself in glory.

When she said as much to Ángelo, he frowned and stalked across the floor towards her, increasing her heart rate just a little bit more.

'I don't care how many times I have to say it. In fact, I'll keep telling you until you believe it, but you are one of the most amazing people I've ever met in my life.' He wrapped his arms around her waist and pulled her close, his fierce scowl melting into a soft smile.

At least this little interaction managed to ease some of the awkwardness between them since walking into the house together. There was no need to try to fill the air with small talk when it was crackling with that sexual awareness again. Looking into one another's eyes, seeing that desire reflected back, and knowing where it was going to lead.

And she wasn't disappointed. Ángelo ducked his head and captured her mouth with his in a tender kiss. Inés's insides immediately turned molten, her body draped around his. In his embrace was the one place she felt content and safe.

He let his hands drift down to her backside, giving her a territorial squeeze, eliciting a little thrill for her in the process. She didn't mind being treated as a possession as long it was only Ángelo taking ownership and it didn't go beyond the confines of the bedroom.

Seemingly with the same idea in mind, he released her and took her by the hand. He led her towards the bedroom at the far end of the villa. Inés followed at his behest into the masculine bedroom. The cream walls and deep red rugs spread on the wooden floor gave the feeling of warmth and intimacy. Rich earthy colours from the tapestries on the walls, to the covering on the huge bed, all contributed to the feeling of a cosy oasis. Somewhere they could get lost in one another and forget about the outside world. All the heat and passion she'd come to associate with Ángelo's touch was there in the decor.

And in his ensuing kisses. He backed her up against the bed until they both tumbled down on to the mattress, tearing at one another's clothes in a lust-fuelled frenzy. Impatiently tugging and unbuttoning, the sound of fabric giving way didn't stop their hurry to have that skin-to-skin contact. It wasn't long before they were both naked and wanting.

The strength of Inés's need for him still came as a surprise to her. Her body responding quickly and fully to his touch until she was aching for him. A throbbing, desperate need which could only be satisfied by Ángelo.

She wrapped her arms and legs around him, pulling him flush to her body, communicating exactly what she wanted. But he seemed determined to drive her to the brink of madness before she found any release.

He dotted barely there kisses along her collarbone and along that sensitive part of her neck which sent shivers all over her skin. The gasps and moans of pleasure and frustration coming from her body were almost alien to her. She couldn't remember a partner ever showing so much consideration, giving her body such thorough attention that she didn't know whether to laugh or cry.

In the past, she'd been the one eager to please, afraid of doing something wrong. Her pleasure had never really come into things. If it happened, it was by accident, not design, and she'd always thought sex was purely for the man's benefit. How wrong she'd been!

If she'd known this was how it was supposed to feel, as though she was the most cherished woman on the earth whose satisfaction was all that mattered, she might have realised Marty was not the man for her before she'd even moved in with him. She was grateful now at least that she knew sex could be something enjoyable for both partners and was an important, intimate part of a relationship. No matter how casual.

Ángelo dipped lower, his hands kneading and caressing her breasts, his tongue licking and flicking around her ever-hardening nipples. That throbbing need for him now like a second heartbeat reverberating throughout her body. And when he tugged on her nipple with his mouth and rolled his tongue around it, she thought she might orgasm there and then.

Lower, deeper, he tended to what seemed like all of her erogenous zones, until he was positioned between her thighs. He lifted her legs on to his shoulders and she held her breath, exhaling loudly when he plunged his tongue inside her. Arousal consumed her, rendered her almost immobile. A slave to everything Ángelo was doing to her.

He showed her exactly how much he wanted to please her. Didn't stop until she was completely satisfied and felt as though she was having an out-of-body experience she was on such a high.

When she finally drifted back and opened her eyes, it was to see him lying beside her with a smug grin all over his face.

'That was…' She had no words to explain what he'd just done to, and for, her.

'I aim to please,' he said with a deep laugh that went straight to her erogenous zones.

'Well, you definitely did that.' She stretched and sighed, rolling over to give him a kiss.

It was nice to share a bed again. Nicer still not to be full of anxiety and worry, completely relaxed and fully satisfied. She traced abstract patterns on his taut chest with her fingertip, enjoying the smooth warmth of his skin on hers.

'Good.' He lifted her hand to his mouth and kissed her. If he hadn't just done what he'd done to her, she might've said he was a gentleman. Thankfully, the bedroom brought out his wild side, even if he still insisted that the lady came first.

'What about you?' Inés slid her hand between their naked bodies and took a firm hold of his arousal, making him gasp for a change.

'Don't worry, I know exactly what I want.' His voice was so deep and gravelly, he practically growled the words. The sound of his heavy desire calling directly to her libido.

Ángelo left her briefly to sheath himself with a condom he took from his bedside unit. Then he was back, kissing her, anchoring her legs around her waist and…*oh!*

That full feeling of having him inside her was

satisfying all on its own, but when he moved, she was in heaven. Ángelo was the whole package, in more ways than one. Not only was he handsome, successful and compassionate, but he was a fabulous lover, too. The fact that he wanted to settle down, too, made him the ideal man for anyone who hadn't been scarred by an emotionally abusive relationship.

For the first time, Inés wished she'd never left Spain. Then she might have met him earlier and they could have stood a chance of both having that happy ever after which had eluded them both so far. Unfortunately, her bad experience meant she didn't want to think beyond the present. She couldn't commit when she was so afraid of losing her identity again. Even though Ángelo made her feel more and more like the Inés she knew she was deep down with every second she spent with him.

Especially when he'd awakened the wanton inside her with such ferocity. She'd gone from someone who thought she could live in celibacy quite happily for the rest of her life to now she couldn't get enough of him.

It made her wonder if there was a possibility they could take the next step beyond the casual nature of their arrangement. He wasn't frightening, or threatening. Ángelo was sexy and loving, and always mindful of what she needed. The sort of person she needed in her life.

So why was she punishing herself by denying there was a future with him? That was letting Marty keep control of her in some way. Keeping a huge part of a normal life on lockdown, afraid that she'd let someone else like him sneak into her life. Except she knew Ángelo was nothing like her ex. He would never undermine her, or make her feel anything less than she was. Especially in the bedroom where he made her feel like a goddess.

He thrust with a grunt. She cried out with pleasure. They could have this every day.

Their bodies rocked together. Once. Twice. Three times. Inés tightened her body around him. Clenched her inner muscles. And Ángelo cried out. She watched the ecstasy on his face. Saw him finally lose control. Finally felt the power she had over him. He was hers as much as she was his. No matter how hard they fought it, they were in this together. Completely and utterly lost to one another. And she realised she was no longer terrified at the prospect.

Wrung out by her emotions and the physical release Ángelo commanded time and time again, her body was limp. All she wanted to do was roll over and sleep. Preferably with a naked Ángelo spooning her from behind. But that hadn't been the plan. She didn't want to push him into something he didn't want. So, with some reluctance, she swung her legs over the edge of the bed and groped around the floor for her discarded clothes.

'Where are you going?' Ángelo was watching her, his head propped up on one bent arm, the bed covers draped tantalisingly across the middle of his body. She didn't have to use her imagination to picture exactly what was underneath when she had intimate knowledge of every part of him. It didn't make it any easier to leave him.

'Home. I can order a taxi if you prefer?' She could understand if he was too exhausted to get her back home when her legs didn't want to work either.

'Stay.' His quiet plea and the cute head tilt would've been enough to convince her to get back into bed, but Inés wanted some clarification about what that meant.

'Why?'

'Because I want you to.' His lazy smile completely seduced her so she didn't care about his motives any more and simply wanted to lie back down beside him.

She sighed at her own weakness. 'What are we doing, Ángelo?'

'Enjoying ourselves, I hope.' He nuzzled into

her neck, completely eroding what was left of her willpower.

'You know what I mean. You've made it clear you want the whole wife and two kids and I'm terrified of getting into anything serious. So where does that leave us if we can't keep our hands off each other?' It was clear abstinence wasn't going to be the answer when she was rewarded time and time again for giving in to temptation where Ángelo was concerned.

He rolled on to his side and fixed her with his deep brown gaze. 'I'm not asking anything of you that you're not ready, or willing, to give, Inés. I just like being with you. Yes, I would like more, but I'm not going to put any pressure on you. That has to be your decision.'

It was clear he was taking her feelings into consideration, knowing the issues she had around relationships. At this point in time she was more afraid of her own feelings than anything she believed Ángelo might be capable of.

'Thanks.'

'Maybe we just need to enjoy this for what it is. Who knows, maybe our next relationships will be better for it?' Ángelo was trying to make this an easier decision for her. Keeping the idea that being together was nothing more than a casual arrangement, even though deep down she knew it had become more than that for her. Especially when the thought of him moving on with someone else, setting up that cosy family environment which didn't include her, was painfully squeezing her heart.

As Inés cuddled into him, relished the warmth of his arm around her holding her close to his naked body, she realised how much she did want this on more than a temporary basis. It would be nice to stay with someone that was making her happy and she had her job, too. Life was beginning to look up for her, but there was a black shadow on the happy scene which she couldn't ignore for ever.

If she was going to ever be able to move on, she had to confront the past first. She didn't want to hide from it, or let it dominate her life any more. It was time to see her father and get some closure before it was too late. Then perhaps she might be able to fully enjoy a life with Ángelo in it, without thinking that he was hiding something from her, and the minute she committed to him he was going to show her a side of him she didn't like. And break her heart all over again.

'I'll see you later tonight. I just have a couple of things to do first.' Inés gave Ángelo a lingering kiss which only made him pull her back for more when she tried to leave.

'I have to go,' she laughed through the kisses.

'Okay. I'll see you later.' He didn't like to push too far in case he scared her away when she was still trying to rid herself of past demons. As much as he wanted something more than the casual arrangement they'd fallen into, he'd rather have her on her own terms than not at all.

Despite her previous protest that she didn't want to get involved so soon after Marty, they'd got into a routine of working and sleeping together. Going out for meals and walks on the beach. They were a couple without the actual label. He was hoping some day she'd feel safe enough to commit to him, but for now he was content to simply have her in his life. There had been no mention of moving away, or looking for work elsewhere, and he got the impression she was happy with things the way they were, too.

Marie was back at work and even she knew better than to comment on whatever was going on in case it upset Inés. Though she must have known when her daughter was spending most nights away from home and the lingering looks Ángelo and Inés exchanged through the working day, when they were waiting to be alone in private, were probably a dead giveaway.

He knew, though, that there was an issue that they all needed to deal with if they were ever going to be able to be together in any significant way. Inés's father.

204 SPANISH DOC TO HEAL HER

Ángelo was worried that if Juan died without ever having reconciled with Inés, that the guilt and regret might force her to move away from the area. After all, she had a history of leaving when she was in pain. Rightly so, but for his own selfish benefit, he wanted her to be content where she was. To have some closure and be able to live her life freely. Preferably with him.

For now, he was simply going to try to keep the peace. Helping out where he could, while still trying to maintain a relationship with Inés and her estranged father. Though he knew she didn't like to hear when he was visiting the hospital. He got the impression it made her feel guilty that he was going to see her father, when it should have been her. But that was a decision he'd learned to leave entirely to her.

It was also the reason he hadn't told her he was journeying to the hospital tonight after work. He'd promised to take some things over for Marie, still trying to prevent her from doing too much in the process. The last thing anyone needed was for both of Inés's parents to end up in the hospital.

When he walked into Juan's hospital room, he was once again struck with sympathy for the man who'd given him a job and friends at a time when he'd needed them most. Pale, arms bruised from having bloods repeatedly taken, and his usually neat hair, dishevelled against his pillow, he looked nothing like the man Ángelo had known for years.

Still, Ángelo plastered a smile on his face and walked towards the bed. '*Hola*, Juan. I thought I'd come and see how you were today.'

'You're the only one who bothers,' he grunted.

Ángelo knew that lying here, knowing his days were limited, he was likely to dwell on all the negatives of his life, and he wanted to do his best to make him feel a little better at least.

'As you know, Marie is under strict instructions to take it easy. She's been doing too much. She's on the mend now, but I said I'd pop in and see you today to save her the journey.' Ángelo deposited the clean clothes he'd been tasked with bringing into Juan's bedside locker and left the sweet treats Marie had made on the table across the bed.

'It's too much trouble to come and see a dying man,' Juan grumbled, clearly having a bad day.

'She has been here twice a day ever since you were admitted. I just thought she needed to rest.' Ángelo wasn't going to mention Inés. With the mood her father was in, he doubted anything good would come of it when she had made no mention of coming to see him.

'You've looked after the business, you're making sure my wife is okay and you're here when I need you. You're the only one who cares, Ángelo. The only one who has ever been there for me.'

'You know that's not true, Juan. Inés and Marie are running the clinic, too. If no one cared, we wouldn't all be running ourselves ragged. Marie will be up to see you tomorrow, on her day off.' Ángelo knew it was difficult for Juan being here, not knowing how long he had left and likely scared that he'd die alone. However, he also knew that Marie needed a break. They were all doing their best.

'And my daughter? She's living in my house, working in my practice and knows I haven't long left. Yet she won't come and see me.'

'It's not easy for her, Juan. She's still hurting.' He didn't want to upset his friend, but he wasn't going to stand back and let Inés take all of the blame.

'Ten years and she won't even come and see me before I'm gone for ever. She's never going to forgive me for the past,' he sighed. 'I only wanted to do what was right for her. Make sure she had a job for life. Perhaps I didn't go about things the right way...' It was clearly something weighing heavily on the man's mind and no wonder when his daughter was so hesitant to see him. However, now having all of the facts, Ángelo could understand her reluctance. She still bore the scars from her past relationships with controlling men who included her father.

'She just needs time, Juan. Maybe if she knew you had some regrets she might be persuaded to see you.' He was torn between two of the most important people in his life. Although Inés didn't want to discuss her father with him any more, Ángelo thought she needed to get that closure for herself.

He also wanted to pacify Juan, too. He needed some reassurance that there was still a chance to make amends with his daughter. Perhaps he could clear his conscience by apologising to her for what had gone on in the past and, at the same time, give Inés some sense of peace, too.

'All I did was push her away. Now she's been forced to come back.'

'It shows you at least that she still cares about you and Marie.' Ángelo knew that her own circumstances had come into play, but it was obvious that Inés loved her parents in some form or she wouldn't have entertained the idea of coming back at all.

'Nevertheless, I've spoken to my solicitor. When I die, the practice will go to you, Ángelo. You're like the son I never had.'

Though he was stunned by the generous gesture, and the sentiment behind it, Ángelo knew he couldn't accept it. Inés was the one who deserved to inherit, not him. Regardless that this was the opportunity for the financial stability he'd been searching for, she needed it, too. This could be her chance to start her new life properly. And it meant she would have a reason to stay. Not only would that be for his benefit, but it could also help her relationship with her mother.

Ángelo had a home and a job—the only other thing he needed was Inés. His feelings were becoming stronger for her and her happiness meant more to him than a boost to his bank account.

'I appreciate the offer, Juan, but I can't accept it. You have a daughter who deserves it more than I do. Inés is a wonderful doctor and she's a great asset to the practice. I couldn't think of anyone better to continue your legacy.'

'I wasn't sure Inés would want to be tied to the clinic when she'd fought so hard against being part of it in the first place...' It was obvious Juan had given the matter some thought, which was evidence enough for Ángelo that this was the right thing to do. He wanted his daughter to take over the family business and Inés would see it was in her best interests, too.

'Inés doesn't always make the right decisions for herself. She might need a little nudge in the right direction on this one, but trust me, this is what she needs.' Ángelo knew she was scared to commit herself to anything after the rough time she'd had with her ex. This was one way they could help her make the right decision.

'If you're sure, I'll contact my solicitor and instruct him to leave the practice to Inés.' Juan closed his eyes as he spoke, clearly exhausted by the conversation, but also looking as though he'd found some peace in making the decision. The one Ángelo was sure he'd wanted to make all along.

'I'll let you get some rest.' Ángelo made to take his leave and caught sight of Inés in the corridor, the expression on her face one of total horror.

Ángelo rushed out after her as she turned away, apparently having decided not to see her father after all.

'Inés, wait!'

She spun around to face him, unshed tears sparkling in her eyes. 'I can't believe I fell for it again. You're just another man who wants to control my life.'

'What are you talking about?' Ángelo had thought he was doing the right thing, sacrificing his own secure future to provide Inés with one. She was acting as though he'd stolen her inheritance from her instead of making sure it went to the right person.

'I went to England ten years ago because my

father had been trying to force me into joining the practice. Now you're conspiring with him to tie me to the place for ever, making decisions about my life without even consulting me. You know what I've been through with Marty and I told you I would never put myself in that position again. I guess you decided you'd do it for me. I thought you were better than that, Ángelo, but I always was a bad judge of character.' Even if she hadn't said a word, it was the tears now streaming down her face that gave away how utterly devastated she'd been by the conversation she'd apparently just overheard.

Ángelo cursed himself for not thinking things through properly before opening his mouth to Juan. He'd been so carried away with securing a stable future here for Inés, he hadn't stopped to consider her feelings about it. Or how it would seem to someone who'd been controlled by men her entire life. He hadn't asked her what she wanted, or let her make the decision whether or not she wanted to stay, and that did make him guilty of trying to control her in some way. Even if he hadn't meant to.

In trying to give her a reason to stay, perhaps make her think about having a future here with him, all he'd succeeded in doing was push her away.

* * *

Blinded by tears, Inés couldn't see where she was going, but she hurried down the corridor regardless, pushing open every set of double doors until she was outside. Inhaling gulps of air through her sobs. The sense of betrayal she felt literally stealing the oxygen from her lungs. She'd come to the hospital with some trepidation, half expecting to incur her father's wrath. Willing to at least try to talk, rather than live with regret for the rest of her life. What she hadn't anticipated was finding out the man she'd given her heart to was as calculating as every other man in her life who'd tried to control her.

They weren't even a couple and he was already making plans on her behalf. After a decade estranged from her father she'd never expected to inherit anything—now Ángelo appeared to have taken control to ensure she did. Deciding that her future was in the practice here in Spain without any consultation, or consideration of how that would make her feel. Tying her to the place she'd run from forever.

Ángelo had made no secret of the fact he wanted to settle down and though he'd been making her wonder if she wanted the same thing, red flags were waving all around. If he was planning her life out like this for her already, just like her father and Marty had, what would it be like for her to be in a relationship with him? She hadn't fled from Marty just to end up in a similar situation, with another man telling her what she could, or couldn't, do. Making decisions on her behalf and not caring about what she wanted. As far as she could see, the only thing Ángelo would get out of this arrangement was having control of the situation once her father passed away. Having control of her.

'Stupid. Stupid. Stupid.' She hit her forehead with the palm of her hand, punishing herself for falling for it again. For getting drawn in with a few kisses and kind words, only to find out the truth once she'd lost her heart. That's why it hurt so much. She'd fallen for Ángelo and convinced herself he could never hurt her the way Marty had.

It seemed she was doomed to go through this time and time again. Falling for the wrong man and discovering when it was too late to do anything.

Someone grabbed her hand before she could hit herself again for being so gullible.

'Stop it, Inés.' Ángelo's voice, calm and quiet, sounded at her ear.

She hated that it still made her weak at the knees.

'Why? I'm so stupid I need some way of making it sink in that I shouldn't get involved with

anyone because it always ends in tears. Mine.'
Inés rounded on him, fired up by anger and
heartache.

He wrenched her hand away before she could
do any more damage. 'What is so bad about
making sure you have a secure future in the
family business?'

Inés couldn't believe he was being so obtuse
when she'd literally just caught him conspiring
with her father to keep her here, knowing the
control issues she'd had with Marty. 'You made
that decision without consulting me, without
asking me what I want.'

'I'm sorry. I thought I was doing the right
thing for you.' He was very good at playing the
wounded party when she was the one in pain.
Just like Marty. Somehow everything was always turned around so it was her fault. Then
she was the one who ended up trying to placate
him, knowing she hadn't done anything in the
first place.

Well, those days were long gone. She hadn't
moved here to make exactly the same mistakes. At least she wasn't living with him and
the sooner she found somewhere else to work,
the better.

'No, you were doing what you wanted, with
no consideration of my feelings. If you'd thought
about me at all, you would've known this was

exactly what I didn't want. I left the country ten years ago rather than take on my father's role. Now you've made sure I can't leave. I'm trapped.' That familiar sensation of suffocation, of struggling to breathe, threatened to overwhelm her. The same way she'd felt every time Marty took control of her plans and told her what was happening rather than let her choose for herself.

'I'll tell Juan I spoke out of turn. You two need to work things out between you. I'll stay out of it the way I should have done from the start. I just wanted to be with you, Inés, and hadn't thought about the consequences of interfering.' Therein lay the problem. Ángelo's natural instinct had been to take control and railroad her into what he wanted.

Whether he'd intended to manipulate her, or not, Inés wasn't going to take the chance of getting involved with someone else who might try to control her. It had taken her too long just to get to this point in her life where she had a say in what happened to her. For once, she was taking the lead and making the decisions about her own future.

'It's too late, Ángelo. I can't afford the risk of getting trapped with another control freak, thanks. Papa can do what he wants with the practice, but I won't be a part of it. Goodbye, Ángelo.' Inés didn't wait to hear any more excuses, or attempts to gaslight her. She'd made the call and she wasn't going to be persuaded otherwise. For once in her life she was making herself a priority and that meant no more men in her life. No more giving her heart away to the wrong people. No more Angelo.

CHAPTER TEN

'MRS ALVAREZ?' Ángelo called out into the waiting room.

There was no response. When he glanced up from his notes he realised why. The room was empty.

He turned to Marie behind the reception desk. 'Shouldn't she be here by now?'

'Oh, yes. She called about twenty minutes ago to say she couldn't make her appointment, so I think you're done for the day.' Marie smiled at him as though she was doing him a favour by cutting short his working day, when it would only give him extra moping time.

'Somebody else could have had that appointment. It's about time we started charging for time wasters.' He couldn't seem to stop the outburst even though it wasn't Marie's fault. It didn't take much for him to get upset these days. He'd been in a constant bad mood since the day at the hospital. Not least because he hadn't seen Inés from the moment she'd walked away from him. She'd even called in a locum to cover her at work.

Marie took off her glasses and set the pen she'd been making notes with down on her desk. 'Ángelo, I don't know exactly what went on with you and my daughter, but it's clear you're both unhappy. You're both acting so out of character.'

So, Inés hadn't told her about their relationship, or what she'd overheard, it seemed. He didn't know if that was a good thing, or simply a sign that she'd internalised everything. If she was in as much pain as he was, he'd prefer she confided in her mother. Even if it did paint him as the bad guy here. He knew how it looked with him convincing her father that Inés should be the one to inherit the business, but he hadn't meant to come across as controlling. His only thoughts had been providing her with the security he thought she needed. And yeah, if he was honest, he wanted to give her a reason to stay. Selfish, perhaps, but he would never have treated her the way her ex had.

It was Inés's fiery nature which had drawn him to her and he would never have wanted to extinguish that fire inside of her. However, she'd made it clear that whatever they had between them was over and he had to respect that. Otherwise he was guilty of everything she'd accused him of.

218   SPANISH DOC TO HEAL HER

'Inés made some decisions and I'm doing my best to respect them.' No matter how painful.

Marie sighed. 'It must've been something serious when she's talking about going back to England to look for another job. I thought when she came back it would be for good. It would make things easier for me when Juan goes to have my daughter around, but she seems determined to go. I had hoped she and her father would make peace, too. We have no way of knowing how long he has left, but it won't be long.'

Ángelo could see her starting to get upset. So was he. If Inés left now without making amends with her father, he doubted she'd ever come back. There would be too much guilt and grief involved for everyone, including him.

She'd come to the hospital that day of her own accord to see her father and Ángelo's interference had likely ruined any chance of a reconciliation. A stain which could never be removed from his conscience if Juan died and he hadn't reunited with his daughter. It also meant that Ángelo would never see her again either and it had been difficult enough without her just for a few days.

He knew they weren't right for each other. That had been apparent from the moment they'd met. Yet, neither of them could deny the chemistry that had sparked between them. The bond they'd forged outside of that with their shared pasts had been a bonus. Despite all attempts to the contrary, there had been an emotional connection between them. They understood one another.

Deep down he supposed he'd been hoping that Inés was the one. That he'd be enough for her to stay, to want a family with him. Instead, it seemed as though she'd been waiting for an excuse to end things. Unwilling to hear him out, or give him a second chance to prove himself that he wasn't like her ex. All he was guilty of was falling for her and wanting her to stay.

Perhaps he could have tried harder to explain that. Waited until she'd calmed down. Told her he loved her. In the end he'd let his own fear keep him from trying.

He'd convinced himself she would have left him eventually, because she wasn't the settling down type. Then again, he wasn't supposed to be the emotionally involved type and look what had happened. He was simply afraid that he'd lost his heart to someone who wasn't going to give him that safe, secure, family environment he'd always wanted. Now he realised he just wanted Inés. Nothing else was as important than still having her in his life and he might just be about to lose her.

'Where is she now?' he demanded, sick of

brooding and wallowing in his own misery when it was of his own making. At least if he knew he'd tried to win Inés back he might be able to live with himself. One thing was sure—if he didn't, he'd never forgive himself. He'd always done his best to make sure he had no regrets in his life. Not following his heart would be the greatest.

Marie blinked at him in surprise. 'I don't know. She's been making arrangements to go back as soon as possible. You know Inés, she's impulsive. She could already be on her way for all I know.'

He hoped not. It was doubtful she'd leave any forwarding address if this was the end.

'Where did you last see her?' He dumped his paperwork on the desk and grabbed his jacket, wishing he had the van with him today instead of his bike.

'At the villa getting her things together. She wouldn't tell me what happened between you two, but I could tell she'd been crying. I know my daughter well enough to know that she wouldn't be upset if she didn't care about you.'

There was a silent plea beneath Marie's concern. *Make her stay.*

He was going to do everything in his power to make that happen. It didn't matter if he had a family, a business, or anything else in his life.

All that mattered was Inés and the love he had for her which scared him senseless.

Inés mentally ticked everything off her to-do list. She'd registered with an agency in the hope she'd get some work by the time she got back to London. With no other option, she'd had to book herself into a hostel. It would do until she found a job and an income, then hopefully she'd find somewhere else to stay. For now, a bed in a shared dorm was all she could afford. Her flight was booked, as was her taxi to the airport. She just had one last thing to do, then she could start yet another new chapter of her life.

A deep breath and she stepped into the hospital room. 'Hello, Papa.'

It had been difficult enough to find the courage to come the first time around, only to have her heart broken by an overheard conversation. She'd debated long and hard about coming today, but in the end, she knew she needed closure. Whatever worries she had that he would reject her, or be disappointed in her life choices again, she would have to set aside for the next few minutes. He was still her father and she didn't want to live with the guilt and regret if she didn't say goodbye to him at least.

'Inés?' Her father tried to lift his head off the

pillow to see her, but it was taking him so much effort, she moved closer.

The speech she'd planned for years to tell him exactly how he'd made her feel, and what a terrible parent he'd been to her, suddenly felt too cruel to say aloud. It was apparent that this was a dying man and the only thing she felt for him was sympathy.

For years she'd been eaten up with anger at her father, picturing the wagging finger, hearing the raised voice and the commands he issued. Now all she saw was her parent clearly in pain and more vulnerable and fragile than she could ever have imagined.

She'd wondered how she would react to seeing him again. Would she cry? Freeze? Instinctively, she found herself reaching out and taking his hand. 'I came to say goodbye.'

'I'm not going anywhere yet.' He pulled off his oxygen mask to speak.

'No, but I am. I'm going back to England.'

She saw the same pain in his eyes as she'd seen in her mother's when she'd told her the news, too. It surprised Inés and she supposed it was a sign of how ill he really was when the anger she'd anticipated was noticeably absent.

He closed his eyes and sighed, as though all the fight had simply gone out of him. 'I had hoped you'd stay. For your mother's sake. And Ángelo's. He's going to miss you, too.'

Inés bristled at the mention of him and she knew she had to say what was on her mind or else this visit was pointless. It was important to get it off her chest when she'd had a lifetime of holding back how she really felt through fear of upsetting someone else.

'I think he can manage perfectly well without me. After all, you said he was the son you'd never had.' Her voice caught on the words, surprisingly upsetting to someone who thought she hadn't even needed to see her father again. Perhaps it had simply been a defence mechanism because she'd known all along he'd only hurt her again, when she only wanted him to love her.

He squeezed her hand. 'I'm sorry, Inés. I'm in pain and frightened and I thought you weren't going to come and see me. That I wouldn't have the chance to ask for your forgiveness. I thought Ángelo was the only one who cared about me.'

Inés hadn't been expecting that at all. 'I just needed time. We never had an easy relationship, Papa.'

'I know. I only wanted what was best for you, Inés, but I didn't go about things the right way. I wasn't always a good father to you and I'm sorry for that. I don't want to die knowing that you hate me.' Tears clouded his eyes. Something she'd never witnessed before and it clutched at her heart. He was trying to clear his conscience and, suddenly, the past didn't matter. Already in so much pain, she didn't want him to carry the guilt of their troubled relationship to his grave, too. It was the one thing she could do to ease his suffering.

'I don't hate you, Papa. I love you. That's why it hurt so much when I could never seem to please you.' Probably why she'd adopted that role again with Marty, desperate to please and always failing.

'I was... I am very proud of you. I just wasn't very good at expressing that. I expected too much. Liked to get my own way. And I didn't know how to deal with it when I didn't get what I wanted. I should never have taken it out on you, or your mother. I thought I was doing the right thing leaving the practice to Ángelo. You never wanted to work there and I didn't want to tie you to it for ever. I wanted to show you I was finally listening to what you wanted.'

The revelation that he'd acted in her interests for once was overwhelming. In his own way, her father was trying to show her he cared.

'I appreciate that, Papa. Mama always said we were too alike. Perhaps I was too impulsive, leaving the way I did ten years ago, cutting off all contact. I should have come to see you sooner.' Seeing how little time he had now, realising that she'd had a huge part in the breakdown of their relationship, Inés regretted that they hadn't reconciled before now.

'You're here now. That's all that matters. I hope you can forgive me, Inés.' That desperation to wipe the slate clean was there in his small voice and the compassion she had for him in that moment wouldn't allow anything else.

'It's all in the past.' She meant it. Being here with him, seeing how frightened he was facing death, she wanted to give him that peace. She didn't care about the practice, or the years she'd held on to her anger. Inés was ready to set it all aside, when she knew this was the moment she'd remember for the rest of her life. That she'd been able to give him some sense of relief in his dying days. In the process, she could forgive herself, too, for the mistakes she'd made along the way.

'Thank you.' He closed his eyes, apparently exhausted by the emotional confrontation.

'I'll let you get some sleep, Papa.' She did something she'd never done before, and leaned in to give him a hug, not knowing if she'd ever see him again.

The feel of his clammy skin beneath her fingers stole away the last of her strength, leaving tears streaming down her face as she rushed out of the ward. Straight into Ángelo.

'Hey. What's wrong, Inés?'

She wished the hands holding her would pull her close, hug her tight and make her feel as though everything was going to be all right. Even though she knew nothing was ever going to be the same again.

Inés swiped away the tears that had fallen and swallowed the ones threatening to show themselves. 'I was just saying goodbye.'

'Are you okay?' Worried eyes searched her face and it would be easy to believe he genuinely cared. But she'd let her guard down too soon and found herself falling for someone else she apparently couldn't trust. Hadn't known as well as she'd thought.

'I'm fine. I have to go.' She attempted to push past him, wishing she'd taken that earlier flight after all. It was going to be harder leaving when the last memory she had was Ángelo being nice to her.

He released her from his grasp, but followed her down the hallway regardless. 'You just saw your dying father and apparently you're leaving the country. I know you aren't fine.'

Inés wished everyone was as transparent as she obviously was. 'We made our peace, now I'm leaving.'

'And you're okay with that? With never seeing anyone again?' Still Ángelo followed her out the exit and into the carpark. He was probably going to sit with her at the bus stop, too, if she didn't tell him everything now.

'He apologised and I forgave him. I think that's more than either of us expected to happen. What are *you* doing here?' It occurred to her that if it was her father he'd come to see he was going the wrong way.

'I've been looking for you. This was a last resort. I didn't actually expect you to be here.' There was that little smile again that made her heart skip a beat. Damn him.

'Not for long. I have a flight to catch.' She didn't know what he wanted to say, but she wanted to get it over with so she could leave. Goodbyes had never been her speciality. Probably because she'd always been afraid she'd be convinced to stay somewhere she needed to get away from.

'Then I'll say what I have to say quickly. Please, hear me out.'

When she reached the bus stop, Inés had no choice but to wait and listen to whatever he had to say. She checked the timetable, then her watch.

'You've got three minutes.' If the bus was on time, which was always doubtful.

'I swear I had no intention of hurting you, or trying to take control of your life. I just wanted

228   SPANISH DOC TO HEAL HER

to find a reason for you to stay.' It was apparent
Ángelo didn't realise the strength of her feelings
for him, when all he would have needed to do to
keep her here was tell her how he felt about her.

Given that she'd been able to make amends
with her father and the life she'd already begun
here in Spain, she suspected Ángelo's interference had simply given her an excuse to call
things off. Because she was scared of how she
felt about him. Because that meant leaving herself vulnerable to getting hurt again.

'I was afraid of getting myself into an all-too-
familiar situation with a man who was going to
take away my new-found freedom. Hearing you
make that decision on my future for me made me
question if I really knew you at all.' She bit her
tongue so she wouldn't say how hard she'd fallen
for him and the pain it was causing her to leave.

'Of course you know me, Inés. You know me
better than anyone else in my life ever has. I've
told you things I've never shared with anyone.
I know Marty hurt you, but I'm not him. I love
you, Inés. And I'm not saying that to emotionally blackmail you into staying. If you want to
go, that's your choice. But I want you to know
how I feel about you regardless.'

Inés tried to stop her battered little heart from
soaring, but it was impossible when he was saying those words she never expected to hear from

him. Ángelo wouldn't bandy the 'L' word about lightly. This was a man who'd avoided relationships until he was sure he could provide a stable home for his future family. Something he was aware she wasn't ready for.

Surely he wouldn't put that dream he had at risk unless he truly loved her? He wasn't trying to impose his will on her, forcing her back home and telling her she was in the wrong here, the way Marty would have. Instead, he was sitting waiting with her for the bus that could potentially take her out of his life for ever.

Inés wanted to believe that she wouldn't find out somewhere down the line that she had got him completely wrong after all and he was the kind, considerate person she'd taken him for all along. She thought of the patients she'd seen him treat, his rapport with her parents and the women at the shelter he helped. Surely they couldn't all be mistaken about his strength of character? Yet she was still afraid to stay in case she was wrong. She couldn't go through another living hell with a man who tried to control her. The only thing that would persuade her to stay and admit her feelings was if he truly put her first.

'I'm sorry, Ángelo. I just can't take the chance of getting hurt again.'

'I understand. I know what you've been through and how my actions must have seemed to you. But I swear I would never do anything to cause you pain. I don't want the clinic, I don't care about a family. I just want you, Inés. I love you. And, if you don't feel the same way, I'll respect that. I'll resign from the practice. I don't want to interfere while you are working things out with your parents, or start your life out here. I won't get in the way of whatever it is you want.'

The plea was there in his eyes. Ángelo didn't have to raise his voice or get physical to make her question herself. All he'd had to do was tell her he loved her, and show her he meant it.

The sacrifices he was apparently willing to make were proof of the extent of his feelings for her. Ángelo was prepared to give up that future he'd been working towards for her to believe in him. All Inés had to do was give him a chance. Give herself a chance to be happy.

'I love you, too, Ángelo. Why do you think I'm so terrified of getting this wrong?' Her words put a big dopey smile on his face, as though he'd never let himself believe that she might feel the same way about him.

He took her hands and made her turn and look at him. 'If you give us a chance, I promise I will prove to you every day that you made the right choice. Please stay.'

It was a plea, not a command, and Inés could almost feel the love radiating from his body to hers. No man had ever laid himself bare to her the way Ángelo was doing now. The only reason she was at the hospital was that she didn't want to live with any regrets and if she walked away now she might be left wondering for ever if she'd thrown away real love for the first time.

'I suppose I could book a later flight if I needed to...' She already knew everything she wanted was here in Spain. Her family, her job and the love of her life she couldn't imagine being without right now.

Then Ángelo kissed her and she knew for once she'd made the right decision. She'd finally taken control of her own life.

EPILOGUE

'Is that all you have?' Ángelo eyed up the couple of bags Inés had sitting waiting at the door of the villa.

'I travel light in case I have to make a quick getaway,' Inés teased, waiting for a thin-lipped response.

'That's not even funny.' He wrapped his arms around her and pulled her in for a kiss. They both knew she wasn't going anywhere but to his place.

'If I'd known, I wouldn't have bothered borrowing the van and just brought my bike.' Once he was done kissing her so thoroughly she would have followed him anywhere, he lifted her bags from the step.

'I guess I'll have to get myself one, too. I don't fancy having to get a lift on yours, or chasing you every morning to work. Maybe we should get a tandem…'

'I will happily walk with you every day if it means we get to spend more time together.' Ángelo put her bags in the back of the van before coming back for another lingering embrace.

It had been six months since she'd made the decision to stay and give their relationship a chance and the novelty hadn't worn off for either of them. That was why she was moving in with him. They'd taken things slowly so they both knew for sure that this was what they wanted. When he'd asked her to live with him she hadn't needed to think twice about saying yes. He'd been there for her through her grief for her father when he'd died not long after she'd had her heart to heart with him.

In those last few days of his life, she and Ángelo had visited every day and even told him they were a couple. Which seemed to make both of her parents very happy. Before he passed, her father had made the decision to leave the practice to both Inés and Ángelo, so they were enjoying a whole new chapter together.

Her mother, who'd inherited the villa and enough money to live comfortably, was still working part time at the practice, but had decided to go to college to study ceramics. Although she'd mourned for the loss of her husband, Inés thought she also had a renewed self-confidence. Doing things that she wanted to do without having to get permission from any-

234 SPANISH DOC TO HEAL HER

one. She was even talking about setting up her own studio.

'I hope you weren't going to leave without saying goodbye.' Her mother appeared behind them, arms outstretched for a hug.

'Of course not.' Inés immediately went to her. They'd grown close over these past months and she was glad they had a good relationship. It gave her a sense of belonging and security to have family she could turn to, as well as Ángelo.

'You know you're welcome at our place any time. We're only a few streets away,' Ángelo reminded them, as Inés and her mother clung to each other as though they were never going to see one another again.

'"Our place". I like the sound of that.' It made her smile that Ángelo was already thinking of it as their home, regardless of how long he'd been living there and paying the bills. Marty had always made a point of saying she was lucky to be living under his roof. Making sure she was aware of the threat he could throw her out on the streets at any time. She knew Ángelo would never do that.

'Well, it is. It only feels like home when you're in it.'

'It might feel even more like that in another six months…' She smiled, unable to keep the secret to herself any longer.

Ángelo frowned, clearly bewildered by her comment. 'What's happening in six months?'

'You know, for a doctor I'm surprised you haven't noticed my symptoms. Nausea, weight gain...'

'I've put a few pounds on myself. I thought we were just comfortable together.'

Inés was really going to have to spell it out, though by the teary gasp her mother just gave, she had at least figured it out. 'I'm pregnant, Ángelo.'

She waited, watching the realisation on his face, before sheer joy took over. 'Pregnant? We're going to have a baby?'

'I know it wasn't something we'd planned, but I'm sure we can deal with whatever is thrown at us. We have so far.' It had taken her a while to get used to the idea herself. There was no greater commitment than becoming a mother and no greater worry. She hoped she would be the parent neither of them had growing up. With Ángelo by her side, she was sure they could provide a safe, loving home to raise their child. They even had a doting grandmother nearby.

'Congratulations. I'm going to be an *abuela*!' her mother said through her happy tears.

Without warning, Ángelo scooped her up and twirled her around. 'I can't believe it. We're going to be the best parents ever. I love you, Inés.'

'I love you, too, Ángelo.' She'd never been so happy, so content.

They were both finally going to have the family they'd always wanted.

* * * * *

If you enjoyed this story,
check out these other great reads
from Karin Baine

Temptation in a Tiara
Tempted by Her Off-Limits Boss
Nurse's New Year with the Billionaire
Festive Fling with the Surgeon

All available now!

Get up to 4 Free Books!

We'll send you 2 free books from each series you try PLUS a free Mystery Gift.

Both the **Harlequin Presents** and **Harlequin Medical Romance** series feature exciting stories of passion and drama.

YES! Please send me 2 FREE novels from Harlequin Presents or Harlequin Medical Romance and my FREE gift (gift is worth about $10 retail). After receiving them, if I don't wish to receive any more books, I can return the shipping statement marked "cancel." If I don't cancel, I will receive 6 brand-new larger-print novels every month and be billed just $7.19 each in the U.S., or $7.99 each in Canada, or 4 brand-new Harlequin Medical Romance Larger-Print books every month and be billed just $7.19 each in the U.S. or $7.99 each in Canada, a savings of 20% off the cover price. It's quite a bargain! Shipping and handling is just 50¢ per book in the U.S. and $1.25 per book in Canada.* I understand that accepting the 2 free books and gift places me under no obligation to buy anything. I can always return a shipment and cancel at any time. The free books and gift are mine to keep no matter what I decide.

Choose one:
- ☐ **Harlequin Presents Larger-Print** (176/376 BPA G36Y)
- ☐ **Harlequin Medical Romance** (171/371 BPA G36Y)
- ☐ **Or Try Both!** (176/376 & 171/371 BPA G36Z)

Name (please print)

Address   Apt. #

City   State/Province   Zip/Postal Code

Email: Please check this box ☐ if you would like to receive newsletters and promotional emails from Harlequin Enterprises ULC and its affiliates. You can unsubscribe anytime.

Mail to the Harlequin Reader Service:
IN U.S.A.: P.O. Box 1341, Buffalo, NY 14240-8531
IN CANADA: P.O. Box 603, Fort Erie, Ontario L2A 5X3

Want to explore our other series or interested in ebooks? Visit www.ReaderService.com or call 1-800-873-8635.

---

*Terms and prices subject to change without notice. Prices do not include sales taxes, which will be charged (if applicable) based on your state or country of residence. Canadian residents will be charged applicable taxes. Offer not valid in Quebec. This offer is limited to one order per household. Books received may not be as shown. Not valid for current subscribers to the Harlequin Presents or Harlequin Medical Romance series. All orders subject to approval. Credit or debit balances in a customer's account(s) may be offset by any other outstanding balance owed by or to the customer. Please allow 4 to 6 weeks for delivery. Offer available while quantities last.

Your Privacy—Your information is being collected by Harlequin Enterprises ULC, operating as Harlequin Reader Service. For a complete summary of the information we collect, how we use this information and to whom it is disclosed, please visit our privacy notice located at https://corporate.harlequin.com/privacy-notice. Notice to California Residents – Under California law, you have specific rights to control and access your data. For more information on these rights and how to exercise them, visit https://corporate.harlequin.com/california-privacy. For additional information for residents of other U.S. states that provide their residents with certain rights with respect to personal data, visit https://corporate.harlequin.com/other-state-residents-privacy-rights/.

HPHM25